The Angel's Jig

Also in English by Daniel Poliquin

Fiction
A Secret Between Us
In the Name of the Father
The Straw Man
Black Squirrel
Visions of Jude
Obomsawin of Sioux Junction

Non-fiction
René Lévesque

THE ANGEL'S JIG

DANIEL POLIQUIN

translated by Wayne Grady

Cover design by Julie Scriver.
Page design by Chris Tompkins and Julie Scriver.
Cover image: *Old Farmer*, 1887, by A.B. Frost (1851-1928), pen and ink on paper.
12 x 7 in. Collection of the Norman Rockwell Museum (NRM.2006.15).
Printed in Canada.
10 9 8 7 6 5 4 3 2 1

Library and Archives Canada Cataloguing in Publication

Poliquin, Daniel
[Vol de l'ange. English]
The angel's jig / Daniel Poliquin ; Wayne Grady, translator.

Translation of: Le vol de l'ange.
Issued in print and electronic formats.
ISBN 978-0-86492-867-2 (paperback). -- ISBN 978-0-86492-741-5 (epub). --
ISBN 978-0-86492-838-2 (mobi)

I. Grady, Wayne, translator II. Title. III. Title: Vol de l'ange. English.

PS8581.O285V6413 2016   C843'.54   C2015-906820-7
                                                  C2015-906821-5

We acknowledge the generous support of the Government of Canada,
the Canada Council for the Arts, and the Government of New Brunswick.

Nous reconnaissons l'appui généreux du gouvernement du Canada,
du Conseil des arts du Canada, et du gouvernement du Nouveau-Brunswick.

Goose Lane Editions
500 Beaverbrook Court, Suite 330
Fredericton, New Brunswick
CANADA E3B 5X4
www.gooselane.com

PREFACE

In Canada, which is a cold country, the name "angel's jig" is given to that moment when someone walking or skating on a stretch of ice suddenly loses their footing and begins to beat the air with their arms in order to recover their balance. It's an involuntary dance that invites either admiration, if one manages to remain on one's feet, or merciless laughter, if one falls on one's face. I'm told that this expression is not very widely used, and for good reason: I'm the one who made it up. Just as I made up the rest of the novel that follows.

What I didn't invent, however, is the practice of auctioning off children and the elderly, a practice that was common in New Brunswick from 1875 to about 1925. It essentially involved reverse auctions conducted by the parish's Overseer of the Poor or by a bailiff or some other officer of the court. Although at first glance it seems an inhumane tradition, it may not have been without its benefits: those in reduced circumstance — orphans and the aged — were kept out of orphanages and poorhouses, institutions that at the time had little to recommend them, and found themselves with a roof over their heads and gainful employment; farmers, for their part, benefited from access to cheap labour. These auctions were entirely local initiatives; no mention is made of them in the annals of the law or jurisprudence. I know, because I've checked. Mentioning these practices in the Maritime provinces today draws nothing but blank stares of disbelief, which is all the more reason for talking about them.

Naturally, the characters who populate this book did not exist before I wrote about them. But they do now.

PART ONE

They pretend there's nothing going on, but I know something's up. They don't know that I know, but that's neither here nor there. Whatever it is, I'll be shipping out. Their skulduggery doesn't bother me; they're the ones who are stumbling around in the dark.

And pretty soon, too, I'm guessing. Most likely Saturday or Sunday. Next week at the very latest.

They don't know they're acting strange, but they are. The other day, for instance, the woman smiled at me, which I took to be a bad sign. The only other time she's done that was at New Year's, when I bought oranges for the whole family. The other day was when I soothed a toothache that had been making her life a misery for weeks. All I did was apply a compress of salt and cloves, a remedy so ancient that these poor souls must be the only ones who didn't know it. When the pain eased, she couldn't hide her pleasure. She even managed to squeeze out a syllable or two of thanks. She needn't have bothered for my sake; she smiles so rarely that the slightest twist of happiness on her face only makes her sour expression that much worse. There's so little room for joy in that woman that even the lullabies she mutters to the child at her breast sound like funeral dirges.

Another bad sign: last Sunday, after supper, the husband offered me his tobacco pouch. The last time he did that was also at New Year's. I refused it with a shake of my head, meaning no thanks, I still have some of my own under the bed, in a small tin box. Then he did it again yesterday, after I helped him with the chores. Maybe he thinks that these small gestures will make me forgive him for what he intends to do. No need to get so worked up about it. I've got no right to judge him: I know how hard up they are, I don't begrudge either of them, the husband or the wife. I'd probably do the same thing if I were in their shoes, take me down to Cap-Pelé and auction me off to someone who's better able to keep me than they are.

The children know something's up too, but they don't know what it is. They must've noticed that the woman's cooking hasn't been up to scratch lately, and there's never anything for dessert, and the man doesn't sing in the mornings anymore when he crawls out of bed. The little ones go around looking sad all the time, which breaks my heart; they're too young to understand why the place is suddenly so gloomy, and their parents have no way of explaining it to them, and so there's nothing left for them but a big emptiness that smells like incense at a Mass for the dead. I miss their innocent joy, their happy games, their huge appetites, their good-natured bickering. They're all I've got for entertainment around here, and their silence is like they're waiting for the axe to fall.

One final, unmistakable sign: the woman and the man are speaking normally to me, instead of yelling. I've been living with them for four years, and they're only now beginning to understand that I can hear them perfectly well, even though I've not uttered a word in my life. I'm neither deaf nor dumb; I just don't talk, that's all. It's a promise I made to myself when my mother was still a young woman, before I was even conceived, when my existence was nothing more than spirit. A bit like the vow of silence that monks and nuns take in their cloisters. But for these people, language is the only country they know, the only thing they own, and to them I'm a kind of voluntary exile, which is all right by me.

The problem is, to the people around here, I'm what they call a nutcase: they think they have to talk to me at the top of their lungs and use fancy hand gestures that are insulting to me and make them look like idiots. No wonder my jaw drops if anyone speaks to me in a normal tone of voice, the way they'd speak to someone who has a brain in their head. Take the doctor's housekeeper in Barachois, for example, whose acquaintance I have recently had the honour of making. When we were introduced, she spoke to me so naturally you'd think she was talking to an ordinary man, and right away I wanted to hop into bed with her.

Never mind the parents—the children accepted me for what I was from the first day I got here. So did the house-keeper, and now it's her face I call up when I need something to help me get to sleep at night. (When I was a boy, I invented imaginary friends in order to feel less alone. When I became a man, I loved imaginary women. Real ones, too. Well, one, anyway. Maybe two.) Now that they're up against it, the man and his wife finally seem to believe I possess a degree of intelligence. They still don't know that I speak in my head—that I can speak perfectly well, in fact better than they do. I have an extensive vocabulary that includes several complicated words that are hard to pronounce. I like forming long, winding sentences in my head that you won't find any-where else except in books nobody reads anymore. I've also learned other languages; you should hear me talking to trees and flowers, and to woodland creatures, to fish and birds, wild and domestic, to stones, and all without the slightest trace of an accent. I understand the stories the wind, rain, and snow bring me. As a general rule, however, I avoid conversations with hurricanes and forest fires; I make myself scarce when I see them coming. Finally, I understand the phantom language still spoken by members of my clan. They may be losing their mother tongue and using some other kind of language, but their speech patterns and colourful expressions all come from that long-vanished world. I've inherited this secret knowledge from my mother.

Once, and only once, someone nearly saw through me. She was passing herself off as a deaf-mute, but I'd been playing that game long enough to recognize a fellow performer when I saw one. She was a former circus rider who had fallen on hard times and ended up washing dishes in a tavern in the small port town of Richibucto. She'd also tried her hand at prostitution, but she wasn't much good at it. She was too small and thin; sailors didn't like her short hair, her ageless face, her body smooth as a polished ship's rail. Without her clothes on, she looked like an undernourished twelve-year-old—no breasts, no bum, and her tiny, nearly hairless mound. There was always a faint smell of horse manure about her, too, a professional hazard, I guess; she could never pass a horse in the street without hugging it, kissing

it, and whispering in its ear. The few johns who went with her
when there was no one else around would change their minds
as soon as they saw her in her room's feeble light, and more
often than not would skip out without laying a finger on her,
as if they thought they'd be breaking some kind of taboo. They
didn't like her not speaking, either. She used a sign language
she'd picked up in some foreign country, and no one around
here could understand it.

When I first ran into her, I thought she was an aging cabin
boy who was waiting for his next sea berth, and I agreed to
share his room as a favour to the landlady. But we figured
each other out pretty quick. It was hunting season and I was
away a lot, but the first of the month I got back she offered
to pay me her share of the rent in kind. (I'm skipping over
a few things here, because actually it took us a long time to
work all this out, for her to explain it and for me to get it.) I
refused outright. I signed to her that I only went with women,
and besides, I'd never paid for sex in my life. She simply got
undressed and clung to me with a tenderness that was not of
this world. I made up for my mistake by doing everything
she asked me to do. I couldn't refuse her a thing after that,
and I'll be damned if I even tried. When I finally let myself
go inside her because I couldn't hold back anymore, she'd
already come four times, most of them straddling me like a
horse, and I found her whinnying went well with the horsey
smell. Lying in her strong, circus-performer's arms, I became
a different man; when I slipped out of her, exhausted, covered
with her sweat and her more intimate juices, I knew at last
that life was worth the candle. When she slept, she became
plain again, her brow furrowed and her mouth hanging open.

I'm no prize myself when I sleep, and so in order not to see her or let myself be seen by her, I slept on the floor, wrapped in a small damp rug.

She also knew the secrets of my mother's phantom language. She's the only one who tried to understand my silence, and she almost managed it. But we should never have got drunk together, which is what we did at night, after our tussles in bed. As soon as she got a bit of drink in her, she'd start in on me, asking me who I was, where I came from, what I was doing there. She kept at it, and when I put her off too much, she would sign words at me that made me mad, and which I couldn't get out of my head: "Your silence is a lie, you're no good for anything but a good fuck, why don't you just kill yourself and rid the earth of the useless piece of crud that you are"—all that and a lot more that I won't repeat because there might be ladies present. But despite all that, I couldn't bring myself to stay angry with her. In fact, I was beginning to fall in love with her.

It was her fault I was arrested, although I know she didn't do it on purpose. She was almost caught trying to steal a briar pipe that she wanted to give me as a present, to make up for her drunken harangues. The Mounties wanted to know if she had more stolen goods in her room, and so they followed her home. As soon as they set foot in the door, the senior officer looked at me and yelled: "It's him!" (He recognized me because he'd arrested me once before, a long time ago, for poaching wild turkeys. He'd had to let me go for lack of evidence, which only showed that he was an honest man, for a cop.) The other Mountie, a constable, was less considerate; it was the woman he was interested in. He rummaged through her meagre possessions, demanding to know where she had stolen this or that, throwing her things on the floor and crushing them under his boot heel for the sheer pleasure of seeing her wince. This proved too much for the officer who had arrested me earlier: he told the constable to behave like a gentleman.

They brought me in, uncuffed at least, and left her in the room, although the nastier of the two promised her he'd be back. I never saw her again, but I've often thought of her pale, shame-faced expression, the look of a little girl caught doing something wrong. She stared fixedly at the broken jewellery on the floor, her gaze looking inward as at a long-forgotten memory.

I miss her sometimes, but not so much since I met the housekeeper.

That's another thing: the woman and her husband have stopped talking about me as though I wasn't right there in the room, as people do with old geezers who have lost their minds. Now when they talk about me, they just lower their voices and move away a bit so they can speak more freely, and all I hear are murmurs, which would drive me crazy if I didn't already know what they were saying. They feel guilty about what they have to do, even if they haven't done it yet.

I'd like to tell them in a quiet way that it's not a crime, what they're planning, so stop twisting yourselves up in knots over it. All they're doing is taking me down to the bailiff's office to have me placed in a different home, and that's fine with me, I know the drill; after all, it's how I got here in the first place. All I want to know is when. I need to be prepared, in case the auction doesn't go well. Because if my services don't find a taker, my next address could be the old folks' home, where people generally croak before you can say "senile dementia." The food is abysmal, medical attention practically nil, and most of the inmates decide to kill themselves before they rot to death.

There's even worse that could happen. If nobody wants me, the Overseer of the Poor has the authority to transfer me to another county, where conditions could be even worse. In the southwest, at Memramcook, for example, the poor who are sold at auction usually go to large farmers, more like plantation owners, who pay an annual lump sum to the parish — forty or fifty dollars a year — in exchange for which they can make you work as hard as they like. You get your room and board, but that's it. They take children as well as old people. At the end of the year, the planters pay the parish the same again if they want to keep you on, but if they don't want you anymore, because you're too sick or old to work, they send you back to the auction block. These planters don't care about their workers; they feed you barely enough to keep you alive, and make you sleep in barns all year long, on beds crawling with lice and ticks and what have you. I once met a gentleman on one of these farms who was a hundred and three years old. They had him picking berries and mushrooms when they were in season, and pumping the bellows in the blacksmith's shop in the winter. He didn't dare complain, but you'd have had to be blind not to see that he was sorry to have lived to be so old.

In a way, the auction is a kind of lottery, because you have only a very slim chance of coming out ahead. For example, the person who gets me at this next sale might be the late doctor's housekeeper, a woman whose voice is so melodious, whose diction is so precise, that you'd think she made her living selling beautiful jewellery to the rich. She could bring me to her house on the seashore in Barachois, the former manse that the people in the village call Wild Caraway. She has a car, too, the only one in the county.

I can just see the two of us leaving the auction arm in arm, paying no heed to the jeers of our jealous neighbours. I'd help her climb into the car, and then get in beside her, as the doctor did in the days when she drove him on his rounds. When we got to Wild Caraway, she would draw me a hot, perfumed bath, and I would doze off in it while she prepared a goose or a leg of lamb served with white kidney beans and a medium Bordeaux. To spare her any fuss, I would tell her, in sign language, not to send my clothes to the laundry, I've seen to it, no need to send them out. She would reply: "Call me *tu* with your hands." Yes, of course I will, I've been doing that ever since I first wanted to taste you...

After my bath, she would rub my skin with one of the late doctor's favourite lotions — Florida Water, maybe — and of course I would return the favour. Our bodies would be stirred by desire, which rejuvenates the flesh and eliminates wrinkles caused by years of neglect and the tyranny of shame. No lovemaking on this first night, though; we'd take our own sweet time, but there'd be no harm in holding hands from time to time in the parlour, as she talked in a gentle way about the joys that come so unexpectedly after a certain age that they seem almost sinful. Which is another of life's little tricks, a secret known only to those who have lived and survived. I'd nod my head and give her a knowing look. After dinner, we would take our tea in the parlour with a glass of cordial (I'm pretty sure that's what she would call it), and then we'd retire to our separate rooms, saving ourselves for the next day. We'd lived only as human beings for so long, it would take us a while to remember what it's like to be a man and a woman. In the morning, though, when the creaking of the old four-poster accompanies the thrill of playful flesh, I would translate my lascivious thoughts into signs of tenderness, and she would do the same, except she'd be a lot more fluent than me.

But I'm getting carried away, and that only brings bad luck. I should know better than that.

Because I could just as easily end up with a family that takes no pleasure at all from life, that thinks eating next to nothing is good for the digestion. Or I could go to a house where it's so dark, you can't tell whether it's day or night. I've known such places, where the old boarder they pick up at auction is nothing to them but an easy source of income, and they resent every mouthful of food you swallow because you're eating away at their profits.

I know what I would do if I ever found myself in a miserable hellhole like that: I'd fly the coop before you could say "Jack Flash." It might be dangerous living on the loose—I've done it before—with the Mounties allowed to arrest me for vagrancy, and farmers setting their half-wild dogs on me, but I've got a few tricks up my sleeve. The next time, I might hide in a large city, for example, where everyone is invisible, Montreal maybe. Or I might lie low in a cabin deep in the Haute-Aboujagane bush, where no one dares to go. My plans are laid out, but I'd prefer not to have to resort to them. It seems to me I'd be better off in a nice house with a woman who needs me for companionship. If it's not too much trouble, that is. I've never been one to ask for much.

I used to like living on my own, but not anymore. I have to admit, I like being around people. Me, the cocksure loner, ends up giving in to the comforts of the collective life. I've had it with simply surviving. I haven't given up being who I am, it's just that these days I want to be who I am with other people.

Just now, the woman here asked me for the third time this week if I had any laundry I wanted done. In other words, she wants me to leave here with a suitcase full of clean clothes, so no one can accuse her of being a lazy trollop who treats people badly. She imagines she has a reputation to uphold, poor woman. She'd bend over backwards to make sure my next family — if I find one — doesn't think badly of her. I don't understand this need she has to make a good impression on some invisible stranger who'll never even know her name.

In this parish, the human auction takes place behind the Cap-Pelé church on Saturdays, after the market closes, or after Mass on Sundays. They place the old man or woman on a cart or a trestle table set up for the purpose. In winter, they hold it inside the church.

It's pretty simple, really. To put someone up for auction, all you have to do is go to the Overseer of the Poor. He takes down the name of the person in question, asks for a few other relevant details, and makes you sign some kind of waiver saying you give up all rights and responsibilities for the person you're handing over to him. Whether it's your father, your mother, your uncle, or some other family member living under your roof, this person then becomes a ward of the parish, placed under the protection of the local clerk or bailiff, who then acts as the auctioneer. You can do the same thing with children you no longer want; he can take orphans under your charge or your own children off your hands, no questions asked. His job is to find them somewhere to live, not to sit in judgment over where they came from. If the child doesn't find a taker, he or she is sent to the orphanage or the reform school, depending on their age. I remember a family that lived on a concession road not far from here; the parents had fourteen children, the oldest being fifteen. They had so much trouble feeding them, they had to put the four oldest up for auction. Three of them fetched a decent price—they must have looked healthy and well brought up. One of them even knew how to read and sign his name. The fourth one, though, was a girl, and no one wanted her; she ended up in the orphanage, where she died shortly afterwards. That's probably the reason the husband and wife in my house never breathe the word "auction": they're scared to death that their own children will be put up for sale like I was. One more reason to avoid the subject with me—not for my sake but for the children's. As far as that goes, I wish I could tell them not to worry. I'm old enough to look after myself.

At an auction, a man of my age—I'm a little over sixty, I think—could end up in a family where he has an outside chance of holding his own. If he has any charm at all, or some cunning, and if he has some strength left in his body, he can turn his hard luck to his advantage. That's what I was able to do with the man and woman here. But it's equally the case that you can end up spending the rest of your days with someone who treats you no better than you'd be treated in an old folks' home. But at least there's a chance you won't.

If I don't get taken in by a decent family, I'll take off. All I need is a little time to make some kind of hiding place down by the river, where I can stash my kit: a couple of changes of clothes, my fur-lined boots, my warm waterproof coat, a sweater, and a blanket; as well as some gardening tools and fishing gear and whatever to make snares with to catch small game—pheasants, partridge, hares. I can eat anything—beaver, skunk, porcupine; there's no wild animal I haven't eaten in my life. A little salt and some cooking oil and enough canned food to last me four days without fishing or hunting, while the Mounties are after me, and I'll be fine. I'll have the money I've saved up since I got here, and if I can't live in the bush, I'll hop the first train out of here. You can't always count on Mother Nature to be kind when she gets you by yourself, but I've spent a good deal of time with her, and I know from experience that the only real danger lies in giving in to the crazy thoughts that get stirred up by being alone, to the point where you lose your will to survive and all you think about is hanging yourself from a branch of the nearest tree. Old guys like me kick the bucket like that every year around here.

The worst thing about the auction is the auction itself. Because all you are is an object held up for everyone to look at. It's as if you were naked on a stage, in the marketplace beside the sea, or behind the church, alone up there on your wagon bed that stinks of rotten turnips. In the wintertime, when the sale is held inside the church, the bailiff takes his place, the children and the old people up for sale are arranged in a half-circle behind him, and the spectators sit on the pews up front. The auction can take up to two hours, sometimes more than that. I hate the ritual. Everyone who's been through it hates it.

But a lot of people show up for it, some of them only for the entertainment value. They get there long before it starts, not wanting to miss any of the action. They mill about, talking about this and that, until the bailiff gets things rolling. Usually, they tell each other stories they've all heard before. "What I heard," says one know-it-all, "is that there was this old guy they kept locked in his room all day because he was always grousing. One day he died, and no one knew it for three days, until the old guy's body started smelling up the house. Heartlessness, that's what that was!" Someone else says: "I've heard a lot worse'n that. There was this old woman who still had a bit of money left..." But they all stop talking when the auction starts up.

The bailiff gives a little speech explaining the procedure. He talks fast because everyone already knows how it works. The old ones and the children are put up on the block according to their age. The oldest go first.

The bailiff calls out the first name on the list. Say he's a proper-looking gent, washed and combed, dressed in his Sunday best. Those who take care of the people being put up for auction make sure they're well fed in the weeks before the sale. Horse traders do the same thing; they fatten up their sway-backed horses, feed them oats and molasses for a few weeks to give them good, shiny coats. Everyone knows that trick, and people would be disappointed if the traders didn't bother going to the trouble. If you don't even try to pull the wool over a person's eyes, he thinks there's something else wrong. He'll wait until someone comes along who's made an effort, who isn't insulting his inner skepticism. Whatever you do, don't screw around with the ritual. You have to at least make a show of trying.

So the bailiff says: "Ladies and gentlemen, listen up... This here's Monsieur Porel (let's say). A real gentleman, he is, knows all the card games and can tell your children good educational stories about the old days. He can still split a cord of wood a day if you pay him a bit extra. The parish is prepared to pay a maximum of fourteen dollars a month to anyone taking this fine fellow, Monsieur Porel, into their home. Those who are generous enough to take him must see that he's lodged, fed, and kept clean. Monsieur Porel has a bit of his own money for minor expenses—tobacco, chocolate, and other treats. And he's in good health: you'll never need to spend a cent on him. The family who has him now brought him to the auction because the mother is expecting her tenth child. Monsieur Porel has to give up his place to make room for the little one on the way, so he's not here because there's anything wrong with him, okay? Such things happen (at this point, the audience usually murmurs its agreement). In other words, this Monsieur Porel is a bargain. His former family is sorry to be giving him up. In fact, they're here today to guarantee that what I've told you is God's honest truth, and they'll also answer any questions you might have. They have nothing but good to say about him. So now, ladies and gentlemen, let the bidding begin!"

(Let me point out that Monsieur Porel is not me. That was the name of an old guy I was put up with at the last auction. He seemed like a real gentleman, as far as I could tell. He was the first to go. They took him some distance from here, and I never did find out what happened to him. Maybe he died. I could have used a different name, or even a woman's, because women are auctioned off the same way, although not so many as men.)

The most painful part of the sale comes right after the bailiff's announcement, when the audience is allowed to come up to the cart or the trestle table, or up to the altar if it's inside the church, to examine the goods up close. That's when any sense you may have had of still belonging to the human race—and when you're old, that's the only sense you have left—goes up in smoke. We go back to being like animals, whether we're the buyers or the ones being bought. The buyers crowd around you and undress you with their critical eyes; they're looking for any flaws, see, any weaknesses, and maybe for good qualities too. They do everything but open your mouth and look at your teeth, or feel your muscles, like they used to do with slaves; here, they're not allowed to touch you. But it takes everything you've got to keep yourself from yelling at them, or choking the first one who comes near enough. No, you don't want to lose control, you want to stay steady as a water lily on a mill-pond, as if everything were perfectly natural, or as if it were all happening to someone else. You have to say to yourself: This is just going to last a moment, it will pass, it'll soon be over. If you panic or scare one of them off, there goes your chance of being taken by a decent family. You have to not be scared yourself so you don't scare them off.

Unless you're deaf, the hardest part is hearing what they say about you. The crowd is always judging you, always amusing themselves at your expense, and they talk about your looks as though you've been stripped of all intelligence and feeling. "I wonder how healthy this Porel is," one of them will say. "He looks a bit on the sick side. He's on his way out, if you ask me. I know the parish pays for his doctor's bills and his medicine, but who's going to look after him, who's got time to do that? A sick man's no good for a house or on a farm. Nobody wants a poor old bugger who wets his bed or shits his pants. You couldn't pay me enough to clean up after someone like that, especially if you've already got kids in the house doing the same thing."

"Yeah, but," someone else chimes in who knows no more about you than anyone else, "if he's healthy, he could be a good deal. He can be a real help around the farm — weed the garden, look after the chickens, collect the eggs in the morning, help sweep up, things like that, you know... And maybe you don't want one who's too healthy, know what I mean? The women in the house might not feel safe, eh? If you got daughters ... Because if you have any trouble along those lines, it's the women who get blamed, not him. If you complain about him, people will just say he didn't know what he was doing! I heard of one case ... "

There's always some kind soul who butts in at this point to put in a few words in your favour. "Yeah, but having an old guy like this around the house could also be a good thing, don't you think? A family out our way got an elderly gent who turned out to be a real bonus. More than happy to make himself useful. Always the first up in the morning to light the stove, and he even got breakfast ready. He split all the wood and kept the stove going all winter. In the summer he looked after the herb garden, and in the fall he helped the wife make jam and pickles. And when he died — get this — he left all his money to the family. He was keeping it in a sock, and he left it for the children's schooling. A nice little nest egg, let me tell you. Kindness pays in the end, and that's something you don't hear often enough." The rest of them mumble that if that were true, the world would be a better place, except it isn't ...

I've heard that story about the good old geezer who makes himself useful and leaves the family an inheritance at every auction I've been to. It's just a story that makes the rounds, nothing more. They never give the guy's name, they keep everything vague. I don't believe a word of it. I've never met a family yet who inherited one red cent from any poor old guy they took in. On the contrary, there's been a good many old codgers who let on that they had some money stashed away someplace and would leave it to anyone who took good care of them. But it's a load of codswallop, when you come down to it; they just say that so they'll be taken better care of. And who can blame them? People say anything because people believe anything. By the same token, the story about the old lecher who bangs the farmer's daughters is also made up, the product of someone's dirty imagination. The only story I believe is my own; it's the only one I know for sure.

Someone says *Shhh!* and silence descends on the auction. The bailiff says a few more words about whoever is up for sale against his will.

"Your attention, please, ladies and gentlemen! Monsieur Porel is eighty years old, more or less, a bit deaf, maybe, but very particular about his person. The woman who had him says he washes his own socks and underwear every month; it's a point of honour with him. He comes with his own linen, too, so there's no need to buy him anything. Not only does he not smell, but he behaves himself at table and can get around on his own. He never treated her like a servant, and was polite with strangers who came to the house. The children love him, too, even if he does tend to repeat stories about his childhood, a common fault among the aged. As far as working on the farm goes, he's a bit past his prime, but he does what he can and you can count on him to do odd jobs, like keep an eye on the house to make sure it doesn't burn down when you're at church. The priest will come to give him Communion once a month, and he says his prayers morning and night. I said it before and I'll say it again: Monsieur Porel is a bargain!"

The people have been listening politely. The bailiff is ready to start the bidding:

"Do I hear fourteen dollars?"

People begin murmuring amongst themselves again, giving each other their opinions, telling one another stories they've heard or made up. Soon, with everyone talking at the same time, no one can hear a thing.

The only real question they ask each other is: "Is he worth the trouble?" Some, especially those who have already looked after someone for nothing, will say no, he isn't. You'd think they were jealous of you for stealing nickels from the poor box. People around here are skinflints; even when you earn the money by looking after someone who isn't one of your family, they resent you for accepting charity that costs the Church money.

Others agree that it's never worth it, but for other reasons. The government only wants to take advantage of our generosity. They're always out to get you. These old people should be locked away somewhere far from here, and stop bothering us with their sob stories. Those who say these things only come to the auctions to gawk.

Some old folks will do anything to find a good home. Once, in the parish I'm in now, an old man borrowed a fiddle and started playing it at the auction. He thought he'd get a better place if he showed he could entertain as well as make himself useful. After playing a few scratchy tunes, he passed the fiddle to someone who actually knew how to play it, and sang a few songs to prove that he had a good voice as well. One of them was fairly risqué, as I recall. To top it off, he danced a jig that went on way too long. Poor guy didn't have a shred of talent, and after laughing at him for a while, the crowd started shouting at him to sit down and keep quiet. The old guy got so angry, the bailiff had to stop the session for a while until he calmed down. Everyone said it was the best auction they'd been to in ages. That was saying a lot in this neck of the woods, where no one talks about the past because most of their memories are shameful. Another time, an old woman being auctioned off cried so hard the whole thing was called off. Neither the fiddler nor the weeping woman were taken, and both ended up being carted off to Moncton, where they ended up God knows where.

The stories start up again about Monsieur Porel, a hodge-podge of gossip and sworn testimonies and counter-arguments all flung back and forth. It's like being in a courtroom with ten trials going on at the same time. For his part, Monsieur Porel sits quietly, minding his own business. Which is smart of him.

A woman in the crowd tells the story of a certain widow who remains nameless even though everyone knows who she is. She used to keep up to six old folks under her roof at a time. Her husband died under mysterious circumstances, leaving her without a penny to her name and a gaggle of kids to look after and the farm mortgaged to the hilt. The six old geezers brought in an average of twelve dollars a month each, enough to feed her family and pay off the bank. If one of her boarders died, she'd hustle off to the next auction and get a replacement. She'd even travel to a neighbouring parish if she had to. Everyone knew her; she was well respected for her lucrative generosity.

A few onlookers wade in. "You're right, madame, it does pay to be generous sometimes, if you work hard at it and keep your head about you, like she did."

Others shake their heads. "Yeah, but even so, that old wid-ow had to scrimp and save to make ends meet. Her boarders didn't exactly have her living in the lap of luxury. The meals

at her place were always the same, from what I heard: porridge
and molasses and tea in the mornings; soup and cake for lunch;
beans and rice and as much bread as they could eat for dinner,
but they got butter only on Sundays. Sometimes a chicken or
a roast of beef. But eggs just on Sundays too. The old guys
could have as many oatmeal cookies and as much tea as they
wanted, which was more than the kids got."

It was a miserable life in that house, someone who knows
what they're talking about says gravely.

Others come to her defence. The woman's house was the
cleanest in the parish, they say. No bugs in her beds, no siree,
and not a crumb lying around to attract mice, believe you
me. Maybe she wasn't so good at varying her menu, but her
boarders never lacked for a thing. And her kids chipped in,
too, which you don't see all that often. One of the daughters
wrote letters for the old guys; one of the sons helped them make
their beds when they needed it. Her boarders were happy, and
the government inspector always gave her a good report for
the quality of her care.

Maybe so, say her detractors, but with all the care she lav-
ished on her boarders, she neglected her own children. Why
do you think they all hit the road the minute they were old
enough? The eldest joined the navy as soon as he could; the
second got a job in town as a maid; and the others took off
the first chance they got. And they never came back, not one
of them. Sure, the old widow had the whole farm to herself,
and she paid off the mortgage, but what's the good of that?
She was at the end of her tether and all alone. They say she hit
the bottle pretty hard because of it, too, and took up with a
good-for-nothing bootlegger who left his wife and seven kids

to go live with her. And after a while he started beating on her and drinking away all her savings; she had to call in the Mounties to turf the bugger out. So there you go...you can't tell me the game is worth the candle. Because when push came to shove, there she was all miserable and broken-hearted, and no kids around to take care of her. If the drink and the tobacco hadn't killed her, she would've ended up here at the auction herself. And it would've served her right, too, if you ask me.

That's the kind of story they like: lurid accounts of big-hearted women drowning in their own tears, or pensioners diddling little children when no one's looking, or poor old buggers dying from either neglect or overwork. When people are in the mood for these kinds of stories, don't bother trying to remind them of the happy family who inherited some old white-beard's sockful of gold coins. Imaginations around here get more fired up by accounts of bad deeds going unpunished, and good deeds bringing ruin down on people's heads.

"Fourteen dollars! Who'll take him for less?" Fourteen dollars is a lot, but the figure goes down fast. The poor old geezer up on the block is facing a crowd with a gift for mental calculation. No room here for the slow-witted or for bleeding hearts.

The first bid comes in barely audibly, stifled as it is by the lingering shame of having to place a price on a human head. They can't see who the bidder is, but they respect him for being braver than the rest. "Thirteen eighty," he says. At this, the rumour mill picks up again, set in motion by those who came mostly for a good show. "You know what I heard?" someone whispers to his neighbour, who is all ears but pretends not to be listening. "I heard that this Porel guy takes a nip or two when he's left alone, and when he has a snootful, he gets as randy as a newlywed. Not that he's done anything yet, mind you, but you never know…" Happily, Monsieur Porel has his supporters in the crowd. "Hey you! Yeah, you! Shut your yap! Likes to take a nip — that's a load of bull! And I happen to know from a reliable source that he's got a pretty sizable nest egg that's being well looked after by a notary public who writes to him every quarter…" This brave defender is also told to pipe down.

"Thirteen seventy-five," comes a voice from the crowd. Silence. Another idle bid, someone says. The others murmur among themselves. No more bids come in for a while as the debating goes on. Then: "Thirteen fifty! Thirteen fifty!" The voices become louder, all pretence of shame now gone as the bidders grow more emboldened. The bailiff smiles contentedly, although with a bit of apprehension too. If the bidding goes too low, the government inspector will want to know if poor old Monsieur Porel is being properly looked after. You can't even feed someone on five dollars a month. Whoever wins has to realize a profit from the transaction, so the price has to be high but not too high. If the bids get too low, the bailiff can postpone the proceedings for a month, or even put Monsieur Porel up for auction in another parish. If nothing else works, Monsieur Porel could be sent to the poorhouse. It's a tricky business, this auction, when all is said and done. A bailiff has to be quick on his feet and have a good heart.

"Twelve dollars," someone says. Danger looms. Suddenly everyone stops talking and starts thinking so loudly you can almost hear their thoughts, which are hardly secret anyway. That bloody Porel, one of them says between his teeth. He might look all right now, but an old guy like that can go downhill pretty fast. They're like children—all smiles one day and stab you in the back the next. He could be hiding a whole sackful of vices, just like anyone else. People get up, move to the front row to get a better look and take a sniff or two, and leave the auction with the smug look on their faces of someone who has just avoided being stuck with a bad deal.

Monsieur Porel takes it all in, but no one asks him for his opinion. According to the law, he cannot refuse to go with the family that takes him. "What do you make of this supposed bank book of his? Has anyone seen it? Who says he even has two cents to rub together? I'd like to talk to that guy. And even if he does, who's to say he doesn't have a nephew in town who'll snatch the whole sum when he dies...?" Too many questions for tired brains. The show goes on and on. Some of the crowd begins to say, That's enough, let's go home, I don't care who gets him, old Porel. But most stay to the end, if only to see whom he goes home with. It'll be something to talk about later.

Sitting on his chair in the middle of the cart, Monsieur Porel is having a little snooze, poor old bugger. He's had enough too. The bidding is taken up again, the price goes down and down... Surely the bailiff will call it quits any minute. But no, the price drops to ten dollars and sticks there. Silence falls over the crowd. Ten dollars isn't much, but you can always make a bit of a profit if you're careful with his food and get some free work out of him. The silence drags on, it's like the lucky bidder is being congratulated by the others, as if they're saying: Good for you, you got him, now take him home and treat him decently. The bailiff declares that Monsieur Porel is going home with Monsieur and Madame So-and-So. The crowd applauds politely. Monsieur Porel wakes up. The bailiff tells him he can get down off the cart, and the four of them—the bailiff, Monsieur Porel, and the middle-aged couple who have won the day—gather around a table with papers on it and a pen. A contract is signed, like at a wedding, and the bailiff counts out twenty bucks for the couple, two months in advance—Monsieur Porel's dowry, you might say. The formalities over, they all get up and shake hands. Monsieur Porel gets his suitcase out from under the table, which his new owner takes from him out of respect for his advanced age, and the three of them leave the sale to the renewed but maybe a bit quieter applause of the crowd. The bailiff wishes them good luck, then shouts: "Next!"

Sometimes the auction goes off the rails and turns into the kind of spectacle that no one forgets for a long time, and everyone secretly hopes to see again because it livens things up a little, gives them something to talk about afterwards. But at the same time, they hope it won't, because it can break your heart. Like last year, when an old woman, originally from town and so with some manners, refused to leave with her new family. She yelled and screamed so much they had to give her back to the family who had brought her, who'd already been keeping her more or less for free for years. She died shortly after that without ever stopping her crying. Other times it's the family who brings them to the Overseer of the Poor, saying it's really impossible to keep them anymore because they've turned mean or do nothing but whine from morning till night. In such cases the Overseer has no choice but to put them in the old folks' home.

Today, though, the crowd looks disappointed. There's no big drama; no one's bawling their eyes out or laughing their heads off. All's well that ends well, as they say. Monsieur Porel didn't bat an eye. No pouting or yelling, nothing. Conducted himself like a real gent. Of course, there are those who prefer it when the people who are sold off make some kind of scene. They can go home with a new story to tell, something sad or funny they can pass on to their neighbours, a yarn to get them through the next few months or years. The best part is when the bailiff says no to a winning bid because he knows the bidder is broke. The old folks are protected from that, and the bidder is embarrassed, and so he should be. Unfortunately, it doesn't come up all that often. People in the audience have to dig way back in their memories to come up with the last time something like that happened.

Sometimes you have to be careful that the auction doesn't suddenly go completely off the rails. You're perched up there in full view of everyone, stripped of all your dignity, and anyone in the crowd can easily take the opportunity to have some fun at your expense, as if you're a kind of wounded circus bear or something. And if you react, you run the risk of waking up the wild animal that lurks in every crowd. A word tossed out in jest can incite other, more vicious responses from the crowd. Jokes become taunts, taunts become insults, and before you know it, the low delight that the strong take in causing pain to the weak is unleashed with a ferocity you wouldn't believe. The crowd loses all semblance of humanity, a beast is born that'll throw itself on you the minute it smells blood. I've seen it happen—a burst of violence that comes from who knows where, like a forest fire sparked by a flash of lightning, and in the blink of an eye the auction turns into a public lynching. And all brought on by the facelessness guaranteed in all crowds. One person's guilt gets sucked into the multitude and is erased from human memory. Then the animal that sprang from the crowd disappears as soon as the crowd does, and everyone goes back to being an innocent bystander who denies being incited to murder by an old geezer who couldn't keep his mouth shut.

I'm ashamed to admit it, but I went to a lot of auctions when I was young. I was the same as everyone else: I wanted to see, to witness a big event, and I hated myself for it every time I gave in to the temptation. Because I really was like everyone else—I felt I was lowering myself to their level.

The worst I ever saw was at a county fair in Painsec that doubled as a human auction. The first day, there were the usual prizes for best sheep, best pig, and all the other animals, with meat sellers roped in to be the judges. A lot of under-the-table alcohol was drunk, which for some reason no one took into account at the time. This was a child auction, and one of the kids being put up had a harelip. The poor guy had been fitted out in clothes that were too big for him, too, and they made him look like a clown. Some of the older kids started making fun of him. He got mad and swore at them in his lisping voice, and before anyone knew what was what, there were beer bottles and rocks flying through the air and the crowd was rushing the auction stand. The parish constable tried to defend the orphans, and was beaten to a pulp by bystanders who'd been innocent as lambs the minute before and whose names were promptly forgotten when the fight was over. The orphans all ran off, some of them disappearing for good in the crowd that sucked everything into itself.

I hope nothing like that happens at my auction. Deep down, people around here are okay, and I know the bailiff. He's an honest man, with an unchallengeable air of authority, and strong as a bull. It's possible that the respect he's shown comes partly from the fact that a lot of people owe him money. All the same, the idea of being judged and juried by the crowd scares the bejesus out of me.

In any case, so long, Porel! Or maybe see you next time!

PART TWO

I don't know why, but lately I'm not as worried about being auctioned off as I should be. Probably because I know there are worse things in life to worry about.

I spent four years in a mental hospital in Saint John, and a couple more in prison, part of it in the penitentiary in Dorchester. The mental hospital was the worst, because I didn't know if I'd ever get out. In prison, at least you more or less know the date of your release, as long as you don't step on anyone's toes. But all it takes to keep you locked up in the loony bin forever is for one person in authority over you to question your mental stability, and just about everybody there is a person in authority over you: administrators, guards, doctors...All the person has to do is get the court to declare you a ward of the lieutenant-governor of the province. He must be a nice guy, this lieutenant-governor—I've never laid eyes on him—to give you this free room and board. The problem is, he can keep you there until the doctors decide you are no longer a menace to yourself or others. And there are a lot fewer doctors there than persons in authority. It's like living in a house with forty doors, all locked, and only two or three keys, and only some of the doors open, and you never know which ones. And usually the doctor who ends up examining you already has an opinion about you based on gossip, or whatever bullshit the guards or the director have put in your file.

So you've got to go around looking as though you wouldn't harm a flea. If you lose your temper even once, your punishment is swift: the isolation cell or shock therapy. After that, they put you on drugs that turn you into a robot, and before long you begin to believe that you really do need to be there. Lucky for me that, when I was there, I was the picture of innocence, more than I'd ever been in my life. The lieutenant-governor, whose name I still don't know, never had a more innocent guest. For four years I lost any hope I might have had of living with freedom and dignity.

The administrators knew from the get-go that I wasn't a threat to anyone. I was there to undergo some tests, I was just there to take part in some kind of study. But I refused to speak, and that made them suspicious. The only doctor I saw when I got there thought my mutism was caused by some terrible thing that must have happened to me when I was a child, and he wanted to get to the bottom of it before letting me go. I'm not sure what happened after that; this doctor disappeared in a puff of smoke shortly after my arrival, and everyone else sort of forgot I was there. The guards tried to teach me to talk a few times, maybe out of sheer kindness, or maybe to have some fun with me, it's hard to say. Anyway, they gave it up after a while and got used to my silence. They didn't leave off teasing me, though. But I didn't react, water off a duck's back, and after a year or so the teasing stopped. I carried out all the chores they gave me without a murmur of protest: cleaning toilets, cutting the grass in the summer, looking after the flower beds, shovelling snow off the walkways in the winter, peeling potatoes and scrubbing pots when I was on the kitchen brigade. I was strong enough to defend myself against the seriously deranged patients, but I never laid a finger on anyone. I didn't even think about escaping, because I knew I'd never get out of there alive if I was caught.

When the guards or the orderlies were in a bad mood and mistreated one or another of us to pass the time, I resorted to a trick I'm not too proud of today: I dropped whatever I was doing and started to dance. Alone. Making all kinds of weird faces. If it was a slow dance, I'd pretend I was looking lovingly into my partner's eyes; if I danced fast, I parted my lips and put on the light-hearted air of a real charmer. I'd have the guards in stitches in no time. It calmed them down and made them feel better. I'd know things were okay again when they began keeping the beat by clapping their hands. "Dance, Mime, dance!" (They called me Mime. I had to have a nickname, and that's the one they gave me. It could have been anything, it didn't matter ... it wasn't about me, anyway.) When my audience had had enough and moved on, I escorted my dancing partner to her seat, thanked her courteously, and went back to whatever I'd been doing.

The need to make myself shrink to invisibility on such occasions was sometimes hard to bear. I was even tempted a few times to go to the director and tell him I wasn't really a mute, but I kept that urge under control. I can only imagine the gibberish that would have escaped from my mouth; I'd have made such an idiot of myself that the director would have decided to lock me up and throw away the key. Finally, I was lucky enough to be examined by a visiting doctor who was in charge of making space in the asylum for some shell-shocked soldiers coming back from Ypres or Vimy. He took one look at me and signed the papers for my release.

I've been with this family for four years now. Before them, I lived alone for about a year in the Haute-Aboujagane bush, where I just about lost my mind. I missed other people: the sound of their voices, their idle chit-chat, their smiles, their complaining, their ugliness and their beauty, their smells, everything that at one time I couldn't stand. Living in the bush makes you go wild, and if you do it for too long, you risk coming out of it more wolf than a wolf, with only one desire: to bite someone, mangle them, kill them, hurt someone else in order to feel yourself alive.

I took to the bush after my cabin at Cape Enrage burned down. It had such a beautiful view of the Bay of Fundy and its swirling tides; at least, it did until its rightful owner put a torch to it. He didn't want any more squatters on his land. He'd been putting up with me for the previous ten years, ever since I got out of the asylum, so I can't say he was an impatient man. Maybe he was afraid I'd put up a fight, like the ones who were there before me. And he probably didn't want another squatter taking my place if I ever left. So one day, when I got back from town, where I'd gone to sell my furs and smoked fish, I found the cabin reduced to ashes. My fishing boat was gutted too, totally beyond repair. If the owner had just asked me to go, I would have taken my fishing gear, my tools, my chickens, and my hunting dog and walked away. I would have been able to start over somewhere else. As it was, I had next to nothing. I just left, no sense causing a fuss. The owner was perfectly capable of sending his thugs in to settle my hash. Those guys would have strung me up just for the fun of watching me kick.

It's hard to own your own land around here, and not because there isn't plenty of it. But if you own a piece of property, there's always someone who comes along and wants to take it away from you. Or else the government orders you off it. So people tend to plop themselves down on the first available spot and stay there until someone forces them to move on. We're used to things being that way; it's how they've always been. If it isn't the government and the police, or some God-Almighty landowner with his own army, it's nature that reminds you that you don't belong in this country: a tidal surge carries off your cabin and all your belongings, or a fire sweeps through, or a drought. And so you throw everything you own into a pack and leave, as I have done many times, and you find another place to plant yourself, farther on. You're always between two exoduses.

My mistake was to hide too deep in the Haute-Aboujagane in order to make sure no one would find me. With the little money I had, I was able to buy enough to eat for the winter as long as I eked it out by ice fishing and trapping, but I didn't take into account how hard it is to do that by yourself. After almost a year of living alone, I'd gone through my entire stock of songs, jokes, and anecdotes, gathered over my lifetime. For my whole life I'd been able to talk to myself and no one else. I'd always been able to have long conversations with my imaginary friends, I knew better than anyone how to tell myself stories, some of them memories and some I made up, but there, in the bush, I reached the point where I no longer had anything I wanted to say to myself.

I went into hiding because I'd heard that the police were looking for me again, some old business about a secret still I used to run. Yes, I knew it was illegal, but only because the government said it was; none of my suppliers or clients agreed with the government on that point. It may have been illegal, but it sure wasn't immoral. I made high-quality moonshine from fir or spruce gum hand-picked by yours truly. I was careful to obey all the laws of chemistry, made it no more than forty proof, whisky as pure as holy water on Easter Sunday; you could have baptized your newborn babe in it, or served it in a sanatorium. It tasted healthy, too — maybe a bit bitter, but it was almost medicinal. And if you drank a drop or two too much, you didn't have to worry about waking up an hour later lying by the side of the road babbling like an idiot or crawling around in a pool of your own vomit. My clients woke up in the morning feeling pure, and they wouldn't need to drink again for weeks afterwards. And if someone couldn't control his drinking, I was the bootlegger his mother or wife sent him to. In the summer I made a spruce beer that was so healthy and flavourful that pregnant women drank it and gave it to their thirsty children. And I sold it cheap, too. Despite its high market value, I stopped making hooch when a competitor smashed my still, which I'd hidden up in the hills. So why were the police still hounding me? Because I made good money from it, and the owner of the cabin figured I'd bugger off faster if I no longer had a source of income and the police were on my back.

The cabin in question was deep in the bush, and had once belonged to a well-known and long-dead poacher. It had become a kind of hangout in that all the local poachers had lived there at one time or another, but it was tucked so far in the back of nowhere that almost no one went there anymore, which was all the more reason for me to find it an attractive place to lie low in. The roof was in good shape; the walls, ceiling, and floor were insulated with straw bales, and the windows were tight as a widow's purse strings. Generations of poachers had made the place homey — it was a fine example of outlaw solidarity. There was a stream running nearby, so no shortage of good clear drinking water. One of the longer-term poachers had hung a few pots and pans on the wall, and the cellar was always full of edibles, like turnips and potatoes, dried blueberries and apples. All I had to carry in was some smoked ham, a tub of lard, some dried beans, and a jar of molasses, which gave me enough food to last at least a year, and the only rule was the one that applies to any temporary shelter in the bush: leave it as you found it, well stocked and clean. There's honour among thieves, after all.

There was a cat living in the cabin when I showed up. I never once had to feed him or give him water; he pretty much took care of himself, and he put up with my being there. He was the best hunter I ever saw. He polished off mice and birds with ease, but squirrels were his specialty. He lined their tails up like trophies at the base of a tree not far from the cabin. He also sometimes caught young hares, which he would bring back to me in his mouth, blood still dripping from them, as if he wanted to show them off. A real poacher's cat, that one.

I hardly saw him during the day, but I felt his weight on my chest or between my legs at night. He always took off the minute I stirred in the morning. He reminded me of those guys who pick up women for a night and then leave before daylight. This cat saved my life; without him, I'd have gone completely off my rocker, living alone for so long. I liked him so much, I wish I'd known his name.

It was an extremely harsh winter. Lots of snow early on, then rain, then a dry cold that split tree trunks with a noise like rifles going off. Merely surviving had never been so tough. I almost wished the police would find me, so at least I'd have someone to talk to. I'd lived alone in the bush before, but the other times I always knew it was temporary, more like an adventure in which I had agreed to live on my own. This time, it was no adventure. It seemed as though it was going to be for the rest of my life, like when I was in prison. There were even times when I felt nostalgic for the asylum; I missed all the artist friends I'd made there.

On Christmas night, one of the coldest of the year, a sound reached me from somewhere far off. The cat heard it too: he walked around the cabin with his fur puffed out to twice his size. Neither of us could get back to sleep. I decided to get up and take a look around, to see what might have caused it. I took my sled and the cat jumped up on it; I guess he wanted to see some new faces too. There was the smell of cold ash in the air, and that guided my steps. I walked all night, and in the morning, from the top of a ridge, I saw him at the edge of a frozen pond, sitting beside a fire that had long gone out, with a dog lying motionless at his feet. I slid down the ridge, waving wildly at him as I crossed the pond with His Majesty the cat perched on my sled as though it were a moving throne. The man was so done in, he didn't even reach for his gun when he saw me coming. It was all he could do to nod his head. The first thing I did was put his dog out of its misery with a swing of my axe. After that, I built up the fire and put up my pup tent beside it, got the guy inside, undressed him, and began rubbing him with snow to restore his circulation. When he was warmed up, I dressed him again with clothes I had brought. Wearing my clothes, he looked a bit like me. I let him sleep for an hour or so, then woke him up and made him eat some of the dried venison I'd kept warm under my shirt.

As soon as he could speak, I knew who he was. He'd changed a lot since the last time I'd seen him, but his voice was the same. I was an old customer of his, in a manner of speaking. He had just joined the force the first time he arrested me. And for nothing, really: hunting turkeys without a licence. He'd let me go with a warning. The second time was more serious; it was after this arrest that I did time in prison, then in the asylum. He was promoted to corporal for that. Now I saw from the badge on his hat that he was a sergeant. Maybe if he arrested me again, he'd be made an officer. It looked as if I was good for his career.

I got him out of the tent, took it down, and signed for him to sit on the sled. We had to get back to the cabin as quickly as we could unless we wanted to be caught in the fog.

I had to hoist him up on my back to get up the ridge. The wind was in our faces, and the walk back nearly did us both in. By the time we got to the cabin, the fog was everywhere, thick and heavy, the kind that shows no mercy to anyone out wandering in it. I put some water on for tea, and we ate cold buckwheat pancakes. I helped him take a piss outside, and then he fell asleep on my mattress. He slept for two days straight, the cat lying between his legs as exhausted as he was.

For the next four or five days, I fed and cared for him. He was too busy staying alive to talk about why he was there, but it was obvious he'd been looking for me. It was also pretty clear that he didn't want to talk about it.

When he was feeling better and the cat had finished licking his frostbites, he read me the warrant he had in his tunic pocket and asked me, in his best official voice, if I was the person named thereon. I nodded. Then he stood up and went to throw the paper into the stove, but I stopped him. I knew he'd never find his way out of the bush on his own, that he needed me to take him back. At first he said no, how would he explain to his superiors that the man he'd arrested had dragged him back to the police station perched on a sled like a child who'd been playing outside in the snow? Wouldn't look too good, would it? I had to insist that he arrest me and take me in.

The next morning, when we were about to leave, he told me in a voice filled with emotion: "We'll work this out, don't worry." He promised me I wouldn't go to jail. I would live with him and his family, and he would do everything in his power to prove my innocence.

I wasn't a bit worried. It would take the authorities a coon's age to figure out who I was, since my mother had never registered my birth for fear they'd take me away from her. And that would give me plenty of time to vanish if it looked as though things weren't going well. According to the doctor who signed my release from the asylum, my name was spelled differently in the police records than in the medical files. No one in the administration knew for certain who I was. My sergeant thought that sooner or later they'd have to let me go because of my age.

As for me, all I wanted was somewhere to rest for a while in the company of other human beings, where I would have time to figure out my next move, which would definitely not be back into the bush—I was too old for that. I also wanted a bit of time to replace the stock of provisions I had used up at the poacher's cabin. A bit of time and some rest, that's all I wanted, and if the sergeant could help me with that, I could take care of the rest.

When we left the cabin, I stepped to one side to let him pass, out of politeness. "After you, sarge," I was going to say. I also held out my hands so he could put the cuffs on me. He looked so embarrassed, I was sorry I'd teased him. So I stayed in the lead, and that was how we left, with the prisoner leading his jailer to prison, along with the poaching cat who also seemed to want to take a break from life in the bush.

The sergeant didn't want to put me in the tiny cell at the detachment in Haute-Aboujagane. He decided instead to keep me at his place, with his delightful family. When we were both rested, he suggested a plan of action. He would take care of the business with the still and see that my case file disappeared. Then he would take me to Cap-Pelé, where the bailiff owed him a favour, and they would put me up for auction at one of their annual sales. It was a good plan. I liked the idea of the auction, because at least that way I'd have a chance of finding a quiet corner somewhere and could make a bit of a living for myself. The sergeant also said he'd take care of restocking the cabin before the poaching season started up again.

I decided to leave in the spring. His Majesty was going downhill fast; he'd lived his life. I wanted to go before he died—I couldn't have stood watching him deteriorate. The sergeant's wife, who was exceedingly kind to me, picked up some used clothes at a parish jumble sale and fixed them up for me. She also got me a small suitcase that already had a few miles on it. When I left, I was almost as good as new.

The auction went well. It didn't last too long and I fetched a good price.

I had a hard time spotting my purchaser. Eventually, a small man with a hat a couple of sizes too big for him detached himself from the crowd. He was followed by a woman with a face like a wax figurine. A hateful laugh rippled through the crowd.

As soon as I saw them up close, I felt sorry for them. They both had mouths full of black cavities that had been there for a long time; the difference was that he didn't seem to mind showing his. He even laughed out loud with his mouth wide open when the bailiff counted out his two months' worth of money. He shut up and looked more serious when the bailiff explained the duties he would have as my new keeper. A good many in the crowd followed us around to the front of the church when we left, almost as if they were seeing off a couple after a wedding.

We started walking. The couple didn't own a buggy—I'd been won by two people who were almost as poor as I was. Good thing for me their farm wasn't far, otherwise the new warmth in the spring sun would have finished me off. Especially since I refused to take off my jacket because I thought it would make me look undignified.

The man looked unlucky, the woman like she had married bad luck incarnate, but both seemed inoffensive enough. I'd be all right with them, as they would with me. The mockery I'd heard from the crowd stayed with me like a bad smell, but the man and woman hadn't seemed to notice it.

When we got to the farm, I stepped aside at the gate to let the woman go through first. The man looked at me, surprised, but the woman understood. I could tell by the way she nodded, as if to say, Thank you, I'd say something kind if I knew what to say or how to say it, but I don't, I'm sorry, I'm not in the habit of it.

As soon as I set foot in the house, I felt good; it smelled like my childhood. I thought it would be a fine place to drop anchor for a while.

We were expected. In the house were a man and a woman surrounded by so many children moving around that I could hardly count them all. The woman was so ordinary looking, she didn't seem to be in the room at all. The man looked as though he went around biting dogs. He stared at me for a long time and favoured everyone with the kind of idiotic comments people make before strangers who don't speak the local language. "He looks well-enough dressed for an old guy...And the way he walks, with his back held straight, you'd think he was the one who bought you at the auction! How much are they giving him for the two of you?" He thought himself quite the joker, a manly type, strong enough to laugh at those who were weaker than him.

It was very hot in the house. We all went outside to sit at a table near the well. The woman and her neighbour served us biscuits and a pitcher of spruce beer that tasted pretty good. The children played around us. They too sized me up without being shy, but with them it was because they hadn't yet been taught any manners.

After a time, I'd had enough of the neighbour's stupid remarks and decided to show him who was boss. I took off my hat and jacket, rolled up my right sleeve, planted my elbow on the table, and looked the bugger in the eye. He started backing down in a hurry, saying to the others: "No, no, I'm not going to arm-wrestle with a guy who looks like he's a hundred years old!" But the children wanted to see us go at it, and the more the man made excuses, the more they insisted. It turned out four or five of them belonged to him, and they were the ones who shouted the loudest. In the end he gave in: "All right, all right, if you insist, but don't blame me if I dislocate his shoulder and he can't use his arm for the rest of his life." I beat him so fast, the children thought he'd let me win out of respect for my advanced age. So I rolled up my left sleeve. The man rolled his up too, with a nasty little grin. I beat him again, even faster. That's when he realized I was left-handed, like him.

The children went quiet. The adults didn't say anything either. I put my jacket back on, and my hat, and I lay down like a man who needed to do some thinking. I spent the rest of the afternoon stretched out between two pear trees, until one of the children came to tell me it was time for supper.

The neighbours were gone and the household was a lot quieter. The family sat me at the head of the table like I was visiting royalty or something, and served me first. I astonished them by taking from my suitcase a table napkin encircled by a napkin ring, a gift from the sergeant's wife. I'd never owned one before. The woman washed it every night after that, as if she were in charge of a liturgical cloth.

Before going upstairs to bed, I sat in the corner, pretending to read a few pages of a book of stories I'd had for the past forty years. I don't know how to read, but I'd heard the stories in this book so often that I could put my finger on any page and know what was written on it, and I knew the table of contents by heart: "Puss 'n Boots," "Cinderella," "Ricky of the Tuft"... Every night, I pretended to read a story. It's the only book in the world I can read; any other always gets me hopelessly lost.

Arm wrestling, using a table napkin, reading a book — that was all it took to establish my position forever in that household. I would hear the parents say to the children that I was a gentleman, not some old beggar they found by the side of the road, that maybe I had been someone when I was younger, before some great misfortune had befallen me and brought me to their doorstep. The children instantly showed me more respect than I could have asked for. This must have been the parents' doing, so they could tell the neighbours they hadn't made a mistake in taking me in.

That first day set the tone for the next four years. A new phrase had entered the family vocabulary: "This is how it's done, the gentleman showed us..." They never called me anything but "the gentleman," even though they knew the name I was going by at the time. A few weeks after my arrival, everyone, both parents and all the children, had their own napkins and napkin rings.

The family was in dire need of the income I brought them. In theory, the husband owned the land, but the farm was so heavily mortgaged, and the man had such huge debts all across the parish, that every time a creditor showed up at the house unannounced, he shook like a leaf and his wife shrank into a corner, trying to make herself invisible. Even the children, who were normally as bold and excitable as all kids their age, hugged each other in silence in a way that broke my heart.

One day, one of these creditors, who'd never been able to get so much as an excuse from the husband, took me aside to tell me the family's long list of woes. Maybe he thought I had some money hidden away somewhere and hoped I'd save the family by paying its debts. When he saw that his tale was getting him nowhere, he tried another tack: he told me he'd take me in when the farm was foreclosed, because a man like me, he said, was worth his weight in gold with the fifteen dollars a month the parish was paying for me.

But I was all right where I was. The meals were simple but substantial. The woman let me bake the bread and cook the roasts when there were any. I gave the man a hand on the farm when he needed it, and he was happy to get my help because I could split as much firewood in an hour as he could in a whole day.

I'd never seen anyone as clumsy as him in all my born days, and he was so lacking in gumption that frankly, I found it hard to take. I remember one time there was a hole in the roof over the children's bedroom; when it rained, water dripped onto the bed the three oldest ones slept in. Instead of fixing the hole, he put a sheet of plywood over the bed and nailed a few shingles on it so that the rain that leaked through the roof ran off the plywood onto the floor. All I had to do was go up on the roof and cover the hole with a bit of roofing tar—nothing to it. The children thanked me quietly so as not to embarrass their father. It made me feel good to see that their hearts were in the right place.

I liked playing with them. All kids wake up smiling for no good reason, and these were no exception. Just seeing them made me forget all the bad memories that still haunted me at times. I taught them to add and subtract with a deck of cards, and when they were sick, I rocked them in my arms, or baffled them with card tricks. One of the lads, the youngest, came to me when he had an earache; he wanted me to blow some pipe smoke into his ear. After that, he lay down on the floor beside me and I stroked his hair until he fell asleep. The only thing about them that made me sad was their poverty. The oldest girl's dress had been made from a pair of faded kitchen curtains; the youngest wore one made from an old flour sack, with the miller's brand name still visible even though it'd been dyed and washed a hundred times. Two more children were born while I was there, making eight altogether. They all

slept in the same room, boys and girls, didn't matter, because
the rules said that the boarder had to have a room to himself.

Their predicament was partly caused by the same hardships
that plague us all: winters too long, summers too short, prices
always fixed somewhere else. But most of it was due to the
father's weakness. He meant well, he had his family's best
interests at heart, but the rest of his body wasn't up to scratch.
The first year he was married, he was sharpening his scythe
in the barn and was struck by lightning. Luckily for him, he
was wearing rubber boots, otherwise he'd have been fried to
a crisp. He was never the same after that, according to the
creditor. Everything tired him out, as if the lightning had
sucked all the strength out of him. "All he does now," added
the creditor, trying to sound like a big shot, "is screw his wife.
They say she likes it. It's the only pleasure she gets out of life.
Which in the end is lucky for him: he can rest assured she's
not going to look somewhere else for a provider."

The husband couldn't work more than an hour without
having to take a nap or else sit down and start spinning yarns.
Every night, he liked to tell his children and his wife about all
the good things he was going to do for them when he got his
health back, and they listened patiently, the way you listen to
a story you've heard a thousand times. But they smiled less
and less each time. They'd all fall asleep, one after the other,
from the youngest up to the oldest, and pretty soon the whole
family was gone to bed. I stayed in my chair, pretending to
read stories about little boys who cut the heads off giants so
they could steal their gold. Silence fell upon the house, and
you could hear a pin drop. Suddenly I'd hear the husband

murmuring a few seductive phrases, and his wife replying to him likewise, and after a few minutes the woman would give a loud, satisfied sigh, my signal that I could finally go to bed.

The neighbours, especially those who had lent him money, talked about how lazy he was, and that hurt him more than anything. He did what he could, but because of his fatigue he couldn't get himself organized. When there was something that had to be done, he couldn't do it; and when he did something, it was usually not done right. When he did something right, it was usually not on purpose. Like fathering children, for example.

I never heard his wife complain, though. She more or less accepted her fate as if she'd chosen it herself. But she didn't take the slightest pleasure in her surroundings; she was always too exhausted. She never smiled, ashamed as she was of her mouthful of cavities. She never sang or played with her children either, for fear of being caught red-handed having a good time.

It was mostly to relieve the boredom that I decided to bring a bit of joy into the house. Call it selfish altruism, if you like. One day, a neighbour talked about throwing out a harmonium because it didn't work anymore. I put on my hat and went to see him. I let him know that I would take the instrument off his hands if he would lend me his horse and cart to get it home. In exchange, I signed him I would split a few cords of wood. He caught on right away. If there's one thing I know after all this time, it's that people love it when they figure out what people who can't talk are trying to say. You can get a lot of favours that way. I heard the neighbour say to his wife, with a smile in his voice, that he had no objection to giving his broken-down old harmonium to a poor old sod who couldn't hear it anyway. "Give it to him," said his wife. "It's just been gathering dust for years. Good riddance to it!".

But I had news for them. I knew how to work with my hands, and—luckily for me—the husband had a whole shed full of good tools. He could have sold them for a fortune, he had so many. He didn't know how to use them, but the act of buying tools and holding them in his hands from time to time must have felt almost like working. His tools were as good as new. I spent the whole winter taking the instrument apart and putting it back together again, and making the pieces that were missing, which took a long time. By spring, I had it back in working condition and was playing it as if it were new. The husband enjoyed watching me work, and kept asking me highly technical questions, which obviously I didn't answer.

After that, the neighbours stopped giving me things for free, but they would bring me things they wanted repaired. I charged them a small fee. They quickly learned that if they asked me to do something for nothing, I didn't understand a word they were saying, I was really and truly deaf. But when they paid me, I could fix clocks and sewing machines and sew new soles on boots. I made myself a good bit of pocket money, enough to allow me to treat the children once in a while, and it's why I have some cash on hand now if I have to run away, unlike the last time, when I didn't have a penny to my name.

I haven't actually seen the order to foreclose on the farm, but there is so much tension in the house, there can't be any doubt. The wife doesn't sigh at night anymore, and she cries all day, and the children have conniptions for no good reason and are even sometimes rude to me. The husband looks even more exhausted than usual, and he no longer talks about what he'll do when he gets better. There's been a bad smell in the house for several days, as if free-floating anxiety has an odour of its own. An odour I'm pretty familiar with.

Nothing like a crazy thought to put me back in a good mood, though: the auction will give me a chance to show off my latest acquisition. A three-piece gabardine suit, navy blue with white pinstripes, a cream-coloured shirt, and a tie like no one around here has ever laid eyes on before — purple with green stripes lightly tinged with pink, a real work of art. The suit couldn't look better on me; it's like I had it tailor made. And it's almost new. It belonged to the doctor in Barachois, a man who knew how to dress and who wore it only a few times. My involuntary benefactor died a year ago of heart failure. His family asked the local barber to dress him for the funeral, but the barber had a sprained wrist and asked me to give him a hand. Ever since that business with the harmonium, people around here have been giving me all sorts of things to do. All my life, people have imagined I have talents I don't in fact possess. I've been taken for a poet, a philosopher, a prophet, and a saint. (Okay, a saint only a couple of times.) I agreed to help the barber mainly because I'd always wanted to see inside the doctor's house, which the locals call Wild Caraway.

I also wanted to see how stiffs are laid out in case I was ever asked to do it again.

While we were getting the dead man ready for his final public appearance, the barber tried to make conversation by giving me a rundown of the doctor's life. He was a good man, the barber said at least a dozen times, a very good man. A very good man who, with his many talents, could have made a fortune in the big city, but who preferred to spend his life in the boonies among us ordinary folk. He'd been happily married to a sweet woman who gave him four children, all of whom were doing well somewhere. The poor woman died young. Consumption, he thought, but he wasn't sure. In any case, the kind of disease a proper woman would get. She had a sister-in-law, her brother's wife, who was widowed and not doing too well on her own, and this relation—who was also a proper woman, he kept repeating—moved to Wild Caraway to look after the family during the mother's illness. She came with her only daughter, who was a little older than the doctor's kids, and she stayed on after the wife's death. Everyone in the parish called her the doctor's housekeeper, but she was much more than that: she raised the orphaned children, gave them a proper education, taught them music and how to behave like the upper crust. When the children went off, she could have left too, but the doctor begged her to stay on. He didn't have to ask her twice. "You see," the barber said in a tone that invited admiration, if not reverence, "the woman had nothing but her kind heart to make her living by."

That's when I began having doubts about the barber's story. What did he really know about this family? He himself admitted he'd been in the house only three or four times, and never farther than the consulting room on the first floor. The more I listened, the more certain I was that he was making things up in order to paint a rosy portrait of a couple who had lived under the same roof for years without being married. Which is understandable: people's imaginations are sometimes capable of kindness, I guess, and I'm sure my barber friend was only sharing in the general goodwill towards these two people who were known throughout the parish for their generosity. He didn't want to spoil the couple's exemplary reputation. "I'm sure," he said, lifting the dead man's left foot, "that in his will the doctor remembered to thank her for all those years of unpaid devotion. The poor woman doesn't have a pot to piss in." He said this with a sad smile that looked almost sincere. Of course, he knew nothing about the doctor's will, but that was the only fit ending to his moral fable. All the while he was talking, I encouraged him by nodding my head, but mainly because I wanted to learn as much as I could about the housekeeper. I'd formerly seen her from a distance but had met her only that day, when I came into the house, and I was still in a state of shock.

When we finished what we had to do with the corpse, one of the doctor's daughters came in with some clothes to put on him for the viewing. She also had a pair of brand new black shoes that the doctor had almost never worn because he found them too tight, she said, taking them out of the box. The doctor didn't like anything new touching his skin — but what difference could it make to him now? Stroking the suit with her hand, she said he'd bought it five years before for her wedding, and only wore it afterwards to a baptism and two or three funerals. Which was too bad, because he looked so good in it.

We dressed the dead doctor and took him downstairs to the parlour to set him in his casket. The housekeeper was waiting, her hands joined loosely below her waist, in the posture of a woman who was tired of praying. She was surely more beautiful in middle age than she had been as a young woman. She was wearing her finest clothes as well, as though to make one last connection with the master of the house. Her perfume smelled of unsatisfied passion. (Yeah, I know, this time it was me instead of the barber who was making up anything that came into my head in order to cover my confusion.) When the barber tried to offer his condolences, I signalled to him that our business there was done and we should go. We said goodbye to the gathering and left the house. As soon as we were outside, the barber turned to me and said, "Thanks for getting me out of there...I didn't know what to say...A beautiful woman like her..."

It's true she was beautiful, in her widow's garb. I even began to feel jealous of the dead man.

A week later, she asked me to come back to the house. In a way I was glad to see her again, but I was a bit afraid I wouldn't find her as attractive as I had the first time. I needn't have worried: even dressed less formally, her beauty remained intact. The woman who greeted me on the porch was still all woman. As soon as I laid eyes on her, I knew that my desire for her was real. I was even afraid it would show on my face, and that she would turn me away at the door.

She wanted to pay me. I refused, of course. I don't know if she understood my explanation, but what I tried to tell her was that the doctor had cared for so many people for free over the years, and the small service the barber and I had rendered was the very least we could do to pay him back. She insisted, saying she had paid the barber, which made me refuse all the more haughtily. (It felt noble or something, a poor man gallantly telling a rich woman to keep her money. Refusing money from the rich is a much underappreciated pleasure.) She offered me a cup of tea. I thought she would make me sit in the kitchen, like a servant, and again I shook my head. I gave a slight bow and turned to leave, but she made a small noise with her mouth that sounded like impatience, took me gently by the arm, and led me into the parlour. It had been a long time since I'd felt the touch of a woman's hand. If I'd had a penchant for the stage, I would have pretended to swoon. I almost swooned anyway. On the coffee table she'd set out the tea things: a steaming teapot and a plate of cookies surrounded by a full china tea service and two carafes, one filled with port and the other with a kind of liqueur I didn't recognize. Such luxury!

She asked me to join her on the sofa, and we talked for a while about nothing in particular. I was so overcome with happiness that I kept getting all the usual signs and facial expressions mixed up: commiseration, surprise, astonishment, indignation, amusement. It was as if I had three faces.

After a very short hour, she asked me to follow her upstairs. In the doctor's bedroom, on a velour-covered chair, she had spread out the suit we had put on the dead man, along with the shirt and tie. The cufflinks were on a little side table beside the chair, and on the floor the shiny black shoes seemed to be waiting for someone to step into them.

"At the last minute," she said, "just before the coffin was going off to the church, the doctor's two sons and I undressed him. It seemed a shame to bury him in such a beautiful suit that could still be useful to someone, not to mention the shoes, which cost the earth. The doctor spent so much time on his feet, he was very particular about his shoes, as you can appreciate—he wanted them to last a lifetime. You probably think it was indecent of me to let him be buried naked, but he always slept in the nude. He claimed he was too hot in bed at night, and that sleeping naked was healthier. And he was such a penny-pincher, I think he would have approved of what I did. He never threw anything out, and the smallest crumb that fell from the table would end up in the soup pot. But as there's no one left to wear these beautiful things, and since you are exactly the same size as him, I thought I would offer them to you. The suit would look so good on you..."

She fell quiet for a moment, then added in a nostalgic tone: "I never saw him naked, you know. And then there he was, naked but dead, incapable of doing the slightest harm to anyone, innocent and vulnerable as a newborn... His sons averted their gaze, but not me. I was certain that such a virile man would not mind me looking at his naked body for a while... Forgive me, I'm just being foolish..." I thought this would be a good time to take her by the hand and let her know I understood, but I'm a cautious man, and since she had been smiling as she said those last few words, I felt that any show of sympathy from me would probably backfire. I made do with a brief nod to let her know she could speak freely in my presence.

We sat in the bedroom for a few minutes, she saying nothing more and me bursting with excitement. Not because she was making me a gift of the dead man's clothes, which I didn't really need, but because she had sized me up, taken my measure, and decided I was worthy. She understood instinctively the kind of man I was, physically, and since she had lived for a long time with a man who was the same size as me, I believed for an instant that I could in some way take his place. She might find me pleasing, dressed in his clothes, and want to get to know me better... All this gave me some reason to hope.

To get rid of these lascivious, paralyzing thoughts, I tried to suss out the situation more clearly. To begin with, the suit was much too good for me. Dressed as I was that day, I didn't think I could live up to it. I also felt a certain unease at the idea of wearing clothes that had just come off a corpse whose entrails I myself had removed. And I know this is ridiculous, but I was afraid his shoes might give me cold feet.

The lady insisted I take the suit and shoes, and so I did, mainly to please her. The thought of replacing the doctor in her eyes lasted only a brief second. I just wanted to see her smile again. She had me try the suit on right then and there. I hesitated, but once again I agreed. She left the room. I undressed with a woman waiting outside the door. That hadn't happened for a long time, maybe longer.

She was waiting for me downstairs, in the parlour, and when she saw me dressed as the doctor, she gave a small cry and covered her mouth. Then she turned her head and began to cry. "Dear God, you look so like him in those clothes, it's as though he has come back to life! Oh! You will take them, won't you? And you will wear them often, promise me!" I looked at myself in the large mirror in the hall. I don't mean to brag, but I thought I looked quite a bit better than the doctor, and not just because I was still above ground. I felt as if I owned the whole house, that all I needed was a haircut and my beard trimmed. I'd see to that soon enough, I told myself.

There were, of course, a few touch-ups needed, mostly to the sleeves. The shirt also required a few tucks here and there. The lady wanted me to leave everything with her and come back in a week, but I had a better idea. I'd seen her sewing machine in the corner of the room, and I asked her to take my measurements and said I would make the alterations myself, right there and then, and that way I'd be able to leave wearing the suit. She looked intrigued, and agreed to my proposal. Taking my measurements meant she had to touch me in a few places, especially around my neck, which is what I had wanted all along. I think she knew that. But I kept everything strictly above board. So, alas, did she.

I went back up to the bedroom to change, and when I came down again with the suit over my arm, I went to work. Under her astonished eyes, I made all the necessary changes, and in less than an hour I had the suit fitting me like a glove. "A man who knows how to sew!" she kept saying. "If anyone had told me I would live to see this day!...My, my." Obviously I'd altered the suit myself in order to impress her, not because I was in any hurry to leave with it on. All the time I worked, I was thinking: I'm going to look so good, she won't want me to leave.

The afternoon was almost over. It was getting close to dinnertime, time for me to go. Overstaying my welcome would have been a mistake. I found her so attractive, I wouldn't have known what to say if she asked me not to go, but I couldn't see myself putting the moves on a woman so recently bereaved. I was also afraid that her not inviting me for dinner would be a way of reminding me of my lowly station in life, or, worse, of showing me she wasn't interested in me at all. Therefore, my task finished, I stood up to say goodbye. She spent a long time packing up the things she was giving me, and I took that as a good sign. "You'll come back for more of the doctor's things, and since you are so gifted, I might find a few chores for you to do." I preferred to believe she was saying that out of politeness, and to discourage me from getting any wild ideas.

But I had no wish to leave. I wanted to enjoy the few memories I had just invented, to play and replay them in my mind—and, who knows, maybe invent a few more. But I kept coming up with excuses, promising myself I'd replay the scenes in my head that might have taken place between us if I'd had the courage to shed the diffident mask I assumed whenever I encountered the generosity of others, to punish them for thinking of themselves as do-gooders and of me as one of the weak and needy. (I'm babbling again, it's still my emotions talking.) The long and the short of it is, I would have stayed if I'd listened to myself, but I couldn't take a chance on being rejected, even if it was only because she thought she was doing what was proper. I knew life too well not to be aware that, at our age, love can make us feel twenty years younger, and desire can remove our wrinkles and banish all thoughts of death. But I also knew that disappointment in love can make us act forty years younger, and who at sixty wants to suffer like a twenty-year-old? The pain is much more intense, and we don't have enough time ahead of us to get over it. Late-life love is a risky business.

I couldn't bring myself to shake her hand, for fear of holding it too long. I bowed deeply, and she gave what looked like a little curtsy, and I left with my parcel under my arm, happy as a beggar who has found a fat wallet.

It hasn't been a good day.

This morning, to take our minds off the cold rain that's been falling for the past three days, and maybe to bring a smile to the woman's face — she'd been going around looking like the Grim Reaper for a week — I decided to wear the doctor's suit. But my plan had the opposite effect: no sooner did she see me come out of my room looking like I was about to leave on a long journey than she began to cry. I thought maybe I looked like someone dressed up for his own funeral. The children asked her what was wrong, and she just blurted everything out: "The gentleman is leaving soon," she said, "we can't afford to keep him anymore, we're going to lose our house..." Then the children started crying even louder than she was, and for the first time since I came to stay with them, they trooped over and gave me a hug. Apparently they've grown fond of me, as I have of them. An invisible bond has grown between us, because of our peaceful and happy lives together, the kind of bond that unites strangers whether they want to be united or not.

Of course, I didn't let my feelings show. I've hidden my sorrows and joys for so long, it comes naturally to me. And then there's the fact that this family's situation is a lot more worrisome than mine is. I can always go live somewhere else, find some other nest to settle down in — no big deal, I've been doing it all my life, I'm the eternally migrating bird of passage, belonging to no country but the one my current nest is in. Only death, which for all we know may be around the next corner, will put an end to my wanderings. To all intents and purposes, I am my own country, where I hope I get along with my neighbours. I don't feel sorry for myself at all. But they're in a different boat altogether. The woman, who goes around looking like a servant who is always on the verge of being fired; the husband, who's dead tired before he even gets up in the morning even though he sleeps all night; and the children, who ask for nothing more than just to be children — where will they go when the bailiff seizes everything? No roof over their heads, no ground under their feet, nothing to sit on or sleep in, no tools to work with, nothing to earn a crust of bread with, not even a toy to play with — how are they going to get by? That's what's been keeping me awake at night, that's the worry I've had to hide from them so that they can find the courage they need to go on. For the first time in my life, I wish I could be a rich benefactor with tons of money who could relieve them of at least some of their misery.

I also have the advantage of having some idea of what's going to happen to me. I know, for example, that I'll miss this creaking bed, with its vague smell of rotten potatoes and mouldy straw, and its lumpy mattress that hurts my back so much it takes me an hour to get to sleep at night. I'll miss it all the same, just as I'll miss these other beings who have become so close to me.

* * *

Seeing the children in tears was too painful to bear, and since it had finally stopped raining, I took my cane and went for a walk down to Barachois. An hour later, I was at the seashore. The tide was low. My thoughts were as clear as the cold spring air. It was time to go back, but I wanted to see the housekeeper again. I'm not the kind of person who shows up at someone's door unannounced, but I wondered if it wouldn't be a good idea to show her what I looked like dressed in the doctor's suit with my hair and beard neatly trimmed. A daydream ran through my head. What if, seeing me, she suddenly realized how lonely she was and offered me a job at her place? I don't know what kind of job—as a gardener, maybe, or a valet—any kind of job would do. A well-turned-out lady like her would look much better with a man on her arm. All I'd have to do would be to inform the Overseer of the Poor that I had found a steady, well-paying job at Wild Caraway. The parish wouldn't have to pay for my subsistence any more, and I wouldn't have to undergo the indignity of another auction. After having me around for a while, maybe she'd begin to have feelings for me, maybe agree to some kind of domestic arrangement with her hired help, someone who looked an awful lot like a doctor when he got dressed up, wearing a good tie, a good suit, and the shoes that went with it. Who knew what could happen?

Lost in such reveries, I was staring into the fog drifting in from the sea when I heard a voice behind me. It was her.

"Well, if it isn't my new friend!" she said. "Good heavens! How attractive you look! If I didn't know for a fact that the real doctor is mouldering in his grave, I'd ask you to examine my wildly beating heart!"

She looked radiant, as did her companions, two handsome women her age, who were as surprised as she was at how much I looked like the dead doctor. I struck a modest pose, but deep down I was delighted. The three women were dressed for a walk, and were carrying pails of clams they had just dug up while the tide was out. Their laughter made me think of three young girls who'd recently snuck out of some strict convent.

I'd made a good impression, but it was time for me to go since it wouldn't be right to take advantage of the situation. I could drop by Wild Caraway some other time, when the housekeeper was alone. But she said: "Come with us! We'll have coffee and cake at my place. I made a pound cake yesterday, and I have fresh cream that I can whip up with some sugar and vanilla. It was the doctor's favourite treat. And you can stay for dinner with us afterwards. Oh, say you will!"

I was even more amazed when the two other women said they couldn't stay, they both said they were expected at home. "No," she insisted, "we'll sauté these clams in butter with some parsley and garlic. We'll make a warm potato salad, and I have a bottle of white wine in the icebox. It's the menu we agreed on, isn't it?"

The women again replied that no, they had things to do at home. The four of us set off together on the same path, in any case, and when we reached the crossroads where one set of ruts went off towards the village, the two women left, promising to come back to dig clams and have dinner another day. As I was bowing goodbye to them, the housekeeper took my arm and said, "Don't tell me you're expected somewhere else, you! You are coming with me. I'm not going to let you go home with an empty stomach. Follow me!" I had the housekeeper to myself, and in my mind's eye there lingered the knowing smiles of the two other women. I must have looked like a little boy on his way to his first costume party.

She asked me to light a fire in the grate while she changed. Somewhere in the back of my mind I knew that I really shouldn't be there, and I tried to clear my mind of any carnal imaginings — not out of respect for her, but because I was afraid she'd see it in my face and throw me out like an old lecher. She came back downstairs looking better than ever, babbling on about how the weather was turning cloudy again, and this and that. While she made coffee and whipped the cream, I looked over the doctor's books in his library, and immediately began seeing myself in my new suit surrounded by all the knowledge contained in those books, wondering if someone looking in might assume I was a man of culture and discernment. It was a pleasant thought, but it didn't last long. It vanished the moment I saw my true reflection in the window: it was that of a vain, ridiculous man.

"I hope you like your coffee strong," she said, coming into the parlour carrying a tray. "That's how the doctor liked it, and I confess I don't know how to make it any other way, I've become so used to making it strong. I suppose it will take a while to break all my old habits. To forget the way he liked things done, all his mannerisms..." Her smile turned sad. The more she talked about him, the more she reminded me of a widow, and I tried to feel sorry for her. Which was not a bad thing, because my compassion cooled my desire, and I thought a bit of restraint on my part would be rewarded. The delay might even fan the flames of my own passion, and maybe a little of it would rub off on her.

(I'm not much of a seducer, I guess that's pretty plain to see. I've never seduced a woman in my life. Those I've had the pleasure of knowing came to me of their own free will, because they desired me. I was always too afraid of being rejected to push myself on anyone. I let nature take its course, and I was certainly not going to change my ways now. If something happened, it happened. I wouldn't force it to happen.)

"I hope you like pound cake flavoured with caraway. The doctor loved it that way, and I've come to prefer it too. When you live with someone, you take on their habits, don't you find? It's a way of loving them." She stopped talking suddenly. She did that often: each time she seemed on the point of confiding in me, she seized up and looked frantically around for a way to change the subject. She was always on her guard, and I could guess why. After all, I was a total stranger in her house, even if I was dressed in her dead master's clothes. "Not that the doctor was in love with me, of course, not at all . . . Don't get me wrong. Never!" She corrected herself with what sounded like a genuine laugh.

"Him and his caraway . . . He picked up the habit at medical school — he graduated first in his class, by the way, his colleagues never understood why he let himself be buried alive in this little seaside village — but as I was saying, he learned in medical school that caraway was a cure for flatulence, and he suffered terribly from flatulence, a real tragedy for someone as dignified as he was. Or should I say a tragedy for anyone who spent all their time in his company? My sister-in-law, when she was alive, suffered terribly from his affliction, especially towards the end. It was she who planted all that caraway you see on the property. It grows like a weed now. She put it in just about everything she cooked: bread, stews, salads, tea...It's wild caraway, or field cumin, as it's called around here, but it's the same as the caraway you buy in stores..." She stopped for a moment to swallow a mouthful of cake, which was excellent. I love the taste of caraway. The coffee was perfect too; so was the whipped cream. Sitting in the living room with her, the fire burning, us chatting away, I suddenly felt like a success in life, like an elder son about to inherit the family fortune.

"Do you suffer from intestinal problems too?" she asked me. "I hope you don't mind my asking, but the doctor often said it was a common affliction in men. An observation I found a bit discouraging, if you know what I mean. Whatever the truth of the matter, I must say that caraway wasn't very effective in the doctor's case. He seemed to enjoy passing wind. The louder and smellier it was, the funnier he found it. He wasn't always the perfect gentleman everyone thought he was, you know. He could be quite crude at times. But he did like his caraway."

Her tone changed, and I admit it made me a bit uncomfortable to hear her badmouthing the man whose clothes I was wearing.

"I still have his cigars. Over there, in front of you, in the silver box on that low table. The box is lined with cedar, to keep them fresh. Help yourself, please do. You'll look even more like him. The smoke and the smell don't bother me at all. I got used to it, you know..." They were an excellent brand. "They won't keep forever. You must take one every time you come here. And," she said, getting up quickly to take my empty plate, "do you like Armagnac? I hope you do. He always drank it when he smoked a cigar. He said it made him feel civilized. I like Armagnac too, now — another habit I picked up from him. There's the carafe in front of you. Take it and pour us two glasses. We'll drink to our new friendship. Would you like that?" Yes, I would, and if she had asked me to roll around on the floor like a puppy dog, I would have liked that too.

Whatever Armagnac was, it was good. I'd never tasted anything like it. I'm not what you'd call a connoisseur of fine wines, but a woman I once knew taught me the art of drinking: you have to warm the glass in the palm of your hand and drink slowly, you can't just knock it back like it was a jar of moonshine, just to get drunk. I say that because my hostess drank hers off in three gulps and poured herself another. Before I knew it, she was on her third. Her cheeks were as flushed as they had been on that pebbly beach with her pail of clams, except this time she wasn't smiling. Her eyes had taken on a hard glare, and her voice became husky, almost masculine. She reminded me of a drunk in a tavern, spoiling for a fight; anyone would do, whoever looked at her sideways, even once. I thought the time had come for me to weigh anchor, and I made as if to stand up.

"You want to make your escape, don't you?" she said. "Well, I'm not finished yet. There are things I want to tell you. I'm not the idiot he thought I was! Neither am I the poor relation whom the good doctor kept at his side for thirty years out of charity!" She poured herself another Armagnac and refilled my glass too, with a tight smile. "Yes, the resemblance is complete now: you with your foul-smelling cigar and your phony pose with a snifter of Armagnac. Don't move, you're perfect! The doctor reincarnated. So you're going to listen to me until I'm finished, and I don't give a damn what you think, whoever you are!" So to please her, I sat back down, feeling like the worst

kind of coward. By the time she finished with me, the carafe
of Armagnac was almost empty.

She had a lot to get off her chest, thirty years' worth. I
listened to her intently, as though nothing she said was out
of the ordinary.

The only part of her story that made me feel uneasy was
when, under the effect of alcohol or maybe from being caught
up in her story, she sometimes mixed me up with the doctor.
She said "you" when she meant to say "he," for example, and
her tone often sounded accusatory. She went back and forth
between calling me *vous* and *tu*, as though every now and then
she forgot who she was talking to. In a sense, I had asked for it:
I should never have gone to see her dressed as the dead doctor.

"I come from Maisonnette, originally," she said, "up north. I moved down here to help look after my sister-in-law, who was ill. That was my official reason, but everyone here will tell you that that was just a pretext, that my charity was actually a mask for my neediness. The doctor, whose clothes suit you so well, went to great lengths to let the whole parish know that I was yet another example of his infinite capacity for doing good.

"My second husband had died three years before. I didn't have two cents to rub together, and the only thing keeping me out of the poorhouse were the speech lessons I gave to rich children, who couldn't have cared less about diction. When my sister-in-law wrote to ask me to come down here, I was at her doorstep before my letter of acceptance arrived. I had my eleven-year-old daughter with me, and everything we owned fit into a single trunk.

"My late husband had been a wastrel. He didn't have a kind bone in his body. Hardly anyone came to his funeral, except for a few creditors who imagined I would have the wherewithal to repay them. He had no friends, his family had turned their backs on him, calling him a black sheep, even his three sons from his first marriage didn't bother showing up. You wouldn't have liked him either. He was big, bald, fat, fond of his own foolish jokes and banal observations. He thought of himself as a clever businessman, but every enterprise he went into came apart in his hands. I'd be willing to bet even his dreams were inane.

"You're probably wondering why I stayed with him? He was the last man on earth I should have married, but I accepted his proposal because I didn't think I deserved to be happy, or thought I couldn't afford to wait around for a better offer. I already had my daughter from a union that at least had a promising start, with a lawyer who was expected to go places, a real man's man, the cream of the crop. Unfortunately, he died in a hunting accident a month before our daughter was born. Since I had no money of my own, I had to go back to living with my parents. When my second husband asked for my hand, my parents made it clear that I shouldn't expect many more trains to pass through my station, and that I'd better climb aboard this one if I didn't want to end up alone. I was a young mother on the verge of becoming a dried-up old maid. I agreed to marry him to please my parents. I was a dutiful daughter, always ready to do what pleased others, stupidly thinking they'd return the favour, which of course they never did.

"He was well aware of my situation, he knew I could hardly turn him down, but he was conceited enough to think I found him attractive. The idea that I never would have looked at him twice if I hadn't been desperate never seemed to have penetrated his thick skull. But I'll give him one thing: totally wrapped up in himself though he was, he did try to be a good husband. My mistake was that I was probably as vain as he was. I wanted to be treated like a princess, I thought he was extremely lucky to have me. No other woman in her right mind would have married him. My friends asked me again and again what I'd done to deserve ending up with someone like him. I consoled myself with the thought that at least my daughter would have a father. But even there I couldn't have made a worse choice.

"Marriage to him was an endless series of year after boring year, and shortly after our wedding my younger sister-in-law met the doctor. He was a magnificent catch, everyone said so. Oh, how I envied her. I met him for the first time at their wedding, to which I had been invited out of pity, no doubt, and I saw right away that he liked me. He wanted nothing to do with my imbecile of a second husband, though, and wasn't shy about saying so to anyone who'd listen. I could hardly blame him, in any case, since I felt exactly the same way.

"As I said, my second husband was a born loser, and it cost my parents a pretty penny to bail him out every time one of his ventures went belly up. That was how I lost my inheritance. The idiot even found a ridiculous way to die: a dead tree fell on him, putting a stupid end to a stupid life. I didn't waste a tear on him, neither did my daughter, and I thought my luck had turned for the better when my sister-in-law sent for me.

"She was bedridden when I arrived, and it didn't take her long to let me know how hopeless her situation was. Her illness was slowly killing her, but it wasn't just that: she told me she had married a monster, a man who had 'enormous appetites,' as she delicately phrased it. He couldn't do without it. When they were first married, she was the sole object of his desire, but as soon as she became pregnant, he began seeking satisfaction elsewhere. Anyone would do: servants, patients who couldn't afford to pay him any other way, not to mention prostitutes he took up with when he went into the city on business. He was insatiable. Even when she was sick, he insisted on his conjugal rights, never once asking her how she felt about it. He'd come into her room at all hours of the night. 'He forces himself on me,' my sister-in-law confided to me, in tears, 'and my health keeps getting worse.'

"I'm going to say something terrible: I envied her. At that point in my life, I would have given anything to have had her problems.

"But she had other, even more hideous revelations to share with me. He'd forced one of their young servant girls to have intercourse with him, and she'd become pregnant. She stayed in the house because she was too ashamed to return to her parents. After she had his child, he gave it up for adoption. Shortly afterwards, the girl died of a fever. He had her buried at his own expense. No one asked any questions. The poor child was written off as a hussy, while the good doctor's reputation as a generous philanthropist remained intact. 'He kills women,' my sister-in-law said. 'You are in grave danger here, your daughter too, and my daughters.' That was the reason she'd asked me to come down: she trusted me and wanted me to protect them—her and her daughters—and perhaps even all the other women who came into his sphere of influence.

"You know what? Although my sister-in-law was not the kind of woman to imagine evil where there wasn't any, I didn't believe her. The man she was talking about could not possibly be the one I thought I knew. It was quite simply out of the question. Period.

"The doctor had two qualities that argued against my sister-in-law's accusations: he was generous, and he was funny. A man who spent his life helping the sick couldn't be—*could not be!*—a monster. And a man who joked all the time, who had a quick mind and a great sense of humour, had to be a good man, didn't he? To amuse others, to make them laugh, isn't that thinking about them, about their well-being? Everyone who came into contact with him left with a smile on their face. In college, and later in medical school in Quebec City, he'd earned a reputation as a jolly fellow, famous for his witty repartee, his bons mots, his silly pranks. I myself found his humour so natural, so much a part of him, that it added to his charm without detracting from his seriousness as a man of science. Could this man possibly be causing my sister-in-law so much anguish? And not only her, but so many other women as well? No, it just wasn't something I could believe.

"I was troubled, to be sure, but I soon realized that if I had to choose between my sister-in-law's account and my own impression of the doctor, I would believe the evidence of my own eyes.

"It wasn't long after that that the doctor called me into his surgery. As I went in, an old lady and her son were just leaving. The doctor had handed them some medicine and told them there was no hurry to pay him, and the woman and boy were leaving the office backwards, bowing and scraping and thanking him, practically blessing him. He closed the door, sat down, and told me about his day with a tired smile. He said he was exhausted, wildly underpaid for all the trouble he went to, and so on and so on. I believed him, I swallowed his litany whole, because hadn't I just seen with my own eyes the reverence in which he was held? I wanted to ease the great man's suffering. I can tell you now that I'm a lot less naive than I was then; I believed his fiction because it was to my advantage to do so. All belief is self-interest, otherwise no one would ever believe anything.

"He asked me for my opinion on the state of my sister-in-law's health.

"'I'm not a doctor,' I told him, 'and I'm not at all capable of providing any kind of diagnosis, but I would say that her condition is worsening and that she needs rest.'

"I said that only because I wanted him to stop his nightly visits to her bedroom. He stood up and paced back and forth in the room, hands behind his back, the very image of the conflicted husband and worried doctor. I immediately saw what my role was: that of the kind-hearted, understanding sister-in-law ready to do anything to help. Anything to spare my young sister-in-law from further indignities. It took me a long time to realize this and confess to it, but I wanted to align myself with him in case my sister-in-law's health didn't improve and she died. I was thinking about what would happen to me after her death — there's no use denying it. I imagined myself taking her place, that I could change him, make a better person of him.

"'It isn't easy...' he said after a long silence, 'you know, for a man...'

"I didn't let him finish his sentence. I told him I understood, and that he could count on me.

"'You've been married, you understand our...' he said, raising his eyes to the ceiling like someone used to suffering in silence. I told him I understood that too, and that my sympathy for my sister-in-law extended to him as well. He gave me a small but meaningful smile.

"I stood up to leave, but first turned to him and said: 'You must do what's best for your wife...'

"He nodded and looked repentant, as if to say he understood what I wanted him to understand. I hate to say it, but I was pleased with my performance: I knew in my heart that helping him was helping myself. Do you understand what I'm saying?

"After that, he stopped going into my sister-in-law's bedroom at night. He and I would sit up after dinner having lovely conversations in the living room after everyone else was in bed. We would talk about the newest books he'd ordered from his bookseller in Quebec City, and he'd ask me to play the piano for him, which I did with pleasure. It was on one of those occasions that he introduced me to Armagnac. I was as happy as I'd been in my first marriage. Finally, I was with a man who knew how to make me laugh and think, who always saw the amusing side of things, but could also show that he was a man of high intelligence. I was won over. Every minute we spent together pushed my sister-in-law's revelations further and further from my mind, befuddled as I was with pleasure and anticipation.

"One night, as we were saying good night, he took my hand and placed it against his heart: 'Thank you, my dear friend, thank you for being here. Thank you for being... for being you. I feel as though I've been reborn in this house that smells like a hospital.' I took his hand and kissed it joyfully, then exited as though I were in a play and had nailed my role. It felt so good to feel desirable.

"Until he succeeded in seducing me, he was the most roman-
tic, charming, attentive man imaginable, like an enraptured
lover. Two or three nights later, he opened my bedroom door
in the middle of the night. I wasn't afraid; in a way, I'd been
expecting it. He begged me to let him sit on the side of the
bed. He couldn't sleep, he said. Deep down, I'd known I would
have to wait for him to make the first move, that if I'd taken
the initiative I would always have felt I had betrayed my sister-
in-law. Then, without warning, he took my hand and kissed
it. And he didn't stop there; before long he was kissing me and
running his hands all over me. He begged me to let him come
inside me, in a voice like a little orphan's begging for a hug.
Do you want me to paint a picture of what happened next?
Imagine me pinned to the bed, my arms spread, him lifting
my nightgown and penetrating me without even taking the
time to get undressed. It was over before it started. He jumped
up, tucked his shirt into his pants, and said, 'Thanks, that was
so kind of you. I really needed that.' And that was all there
was to it. Suddenly he began talking about something else:
the horse he had just bought, how it was less skittish than the
one he had had before. Before leaving, he even started to tell
me a joke: 'Have you heard the one about the homosexual
and the vegetarian...?' I don't remember the rest of it. I just
lay there, my mouth hanging open. I couldn't believe what
had happened. He hadn't exactly raped me, I'd more or less
consented to it, but I felt I was less than nothing, a convenient
receptacle for his selfish pleasure. I could have been anyone, it
wouldn't have made the slightest difference to him.

"The next morning at breakfast, he was his old, charming
self, attentive and chatty as usual when he was in a good mood.

That night, he came into my room again and replayed exactly the same scene as the night before. He came to my room every night after that.

"Sometimes, after emptying himself in me, he would lie down beside me on the bed and ask me to stroke his hair. He'd stay for an hour or so, as calm as a nursing baby who'd had his fill. He would talk a bit, sometimes even say nice things to me, and once in a while he would ask me to forgive him. Not often, mind, and I always forgave him, because I knew that what I was doing was for the good.

"Shortly after that, my sister-in-law told me that she was finally being left in peace. She could sleep soundly and was able to devote all her remaining strength to her children. She was almost happy. She died one night when the heat was suffocating. During the following weeks, he ravished me at least twice a night. Without getting undressed, of course, as if he were in a terrible hurry to get something done. Remember I told you I never saw him naked?"

I have to say that as I listened to her story, my feelings for her swung back and forth between repulsion and almost overpowering desire. She had stopped drinking, the Armagnac was almost gone, her voice had become calmer, even soothing. She seemed to find comfort in her own words. By then it was completely dark in the room, the only light coming from the coals glowing in the fireplace. I would have got up and left, but I was afraid of making her angry, and so I sat as still as a post.

"As you can imagine, there wasn't a lot of poetry in our relationship. My only function was to comfort him. For him it was just a game, nothing more. He amused himself with me in a house saddened by the death of his wife and the anguish of his children. Our coupling was a kind of therapy for him.

"The violence came later. Also as a kind of game. It began by his pinching me. With two fingers at the beginning, then later with his whole hand. He said it helped him ejaculate sooner and with more force. He liked to hear me cry out in pain. He said I didn't cry out like a woman in pleasure, so he had to make me cry out by hurting me. Pleasure or pain, it was the same to him. Before long, my whole body was covered in bruises and black and brown splotches. When he asked me if I'd had an orgasm, he would get angry if I said no, so I learned to say yes. He didn't always believe me, in which case he'd slap me, call me names. He called me his cocksucker because I was living off his bounty; he also called me his slutty nurse, his filthy, hairy hole, and I don't know what else. The only way I could make these tortures stop was by crying. Whenever I held back my tears and stood up to him with a certain amount of moral strength, it would put him in such a black fury he'd hit me and threaten to throw me and my daughter out into the street. I'd end up poor, alone, unwanted, he'd drag my name through the mud until the end of time. And so I would pretend to cry, and he would calm down, and eventually leave me alone.

"The death of my sister-in-law didn't change a thing. He didn't shed a tear at the time, although he obviously enjoyed the waves of sympathy he received from the four corners of the county; that puffed him up even further. Before having his way with me, he liked to poke his fingers into my every orifice. At such moments he would get a faraway look on his face, like a child pulling a doll apart or torturing a small animal. It was worse when the children were away and there was nothing holding him back. He would punch me, or kick me if he was in a bad mood, or slap me as hard as he could. What he liked most was when I cried and afterwards forgave him. He liked causing pain and then feeling that he had cured it.

"Of course, I said nothing about this to anyone. There's no one like victims to exonerate their torturers. There were times when I thought he hurt me because he hated the fact that he was sleeping with a woman who was beneath him, and I told myself that the blows he gave me were really aimed at himself. That it really pained him to be causing me so much pain. And so I forgave him, obviously. Not without a little self-interest thrown in, you understand. If I had complained, he would have thrown me and my daughter out on the street, and I would have lost any chance I'd had of his marrying me someday. And so I held my tongue. And it was a lot easier if I forgave him for hitting me, and insulting me, and kicking me, and humiliating me!

"It took me a long time to understand all this. You see, he was someone who had worked his way up the social ladder by being a kind of court jester. He'd charmed his professors and fellow students by playing to the gallery. And once he became a doctor, he set himself up as a kind of benevolent dictator. How could he play both roles at the same time? A king with an irrepressible urge to make fun of his subjects, to use whatever means at his disposal to belittle them and aggrandize himself. And his weapons of choice were laughter and game-playing. I had become his favourite toy. He knew he had me where he wanted me, he'd read me like an open book, and knowing that allowed him to lose all restraint.

"And now, with your permission, my dear friend who never says anything, I'm going to tell you something that still makes me cringe with shame. I loved him; I desired him; I wanted him. And it wasn't just the terror of being a poverty-stricken widow; he was a man loved by a woman from whom love had always fled. He was my revenge on life. I was caught in a trap and happy to be so. I had fallen in love with his projected self the first time I saw him, and from then on I loved the image I had of myself at his side, submissive, generous: the picture of a perfect couple, bound together by dishonesty and indignity, chained to this rotten existence.

"Every time he hurt me with his cruel words or slept with me without loving me, I grew tougher, considered myself more worthy of him than my dead sister-in-law had been. I resolved to be stronger than her, even one day to make him respect me, love me. I decided to let it go on. Decided also to build the nest around him that I myself had never had. That ambition gave me the strength I needed to endure. I thought I could take my sister-in-law's place by his side and use my body to protect my nieces and daughter. You're thinking what an idiot I was, aren't you, my silent friend? Well, you're only half wrong.

"My illusions came to my rescue whenever I was tempted to leave him. I tried to persuade myself that one day, when old age had worn him down, I would overcome his disappointment in me and earn his love.

"But the children's misery made me see things differently. He could do what he liked with me, I knew I was strong enough to withstand it, but my resolution evaporated when he went after the children. He had two sons, both strong and intelligent young men. They were very like him in that, and the resemblance grated on him; he did everything in his power to turn them into docile little ninnies. I remember how he used to hit them with his set of keys. Of course, the poor things could do nothing right in his eyes, there was nothing he wouldn't say to put them down. Always in a joking way, of course, but I could see that it wounded them. The only saving grace was that he came upon them too late. He'd barely been aware of their existence while my sister-in-law was alive, and she raised them well, which was why they were able to resist him to a certain extent. The young men had only got to know their father for a short time, and I did my best to protect them from him. But you see, in protecting them I was also protecting my torturer; I was afraid that one day one of the lads would take a gun and blow the monster's brains out. I convinced him to send them to a boarding school, and it probably saved their lives. His, too. We hardly ever saw them after that. They've moved on, both are doing well, and neither of them is like him, as far as I can tell.

"As for the two girls, it was an almost hopeless battle from the start. They quickly grew into beautiful young women, like their mother, and it wasn't long before he began to take an interest in them. I watched him making his moves, it was like watching a cat stalking two innocent birds. I had to do something. I was at my wits' end.

"And then one day the whole cruel facade crumbled around our heads, like a sandcastle when the tide comes in. Do you want me to tell you how it happened? Maybe not, but I'm going to tell you anyway, so stay where you are.

"We had a guest in the house, a former colleague of his from medical school who was in the area because he was thinking of setting up a practice in Shediac. Over dinner, the happy tyrant was in good form. No one else could get a word in edgewise: his stunts as a medical student, the practical jokes he'd played on his professors, the witty repartee that had made his reputation. Our guest smiled, the children ate staring down at their plates, saying nothing, as usual. Then, all of a sudden, he started talking about something other than himself. He began criticizing the meal: the roast was overdone, the wine tasted like vinegar. I was certain some kind of crisis was coming, that he was going to say or do something terrible in order to impress his guest and make fun of his family's docility. I almost wished he'd insult me and get it over with, let the storm break over my head and pass on.

"In the end, I'm the one who exploded. Have you ever done anything really crazy in your life? I have. Only once, but it was a real zinger.

"He suddenly stopped speaking, as though savouring his own greatness, or else looking for his next amusing topic of conversation, who knows? I knew he would find something, and he did. In his best doctoral tone, he asked his friend if he'd heard of a new medication they were giving to boys who touched themselves, a kind of syrup with anaesthetizing properties, he said, that relieves young men of the urge to masturbate. One of his sons blushed and the other turned pale. Encouraged by their reactions, he went on to say that this syrup, so useful for the peace of adolescents and the purity of families, was sometimes also prescribed to young women, although in somewhat smaller doses. The two boys were trembling with humiliation. The girls were disgusted. But he—he was triumphant, his face shone with delight, finally happy that he had embarrassed and shamed everyone at the table.

"I stood up and said to our guest, who looked as though he wanted to sink through the floor: 'My dear doctor, you know how your colleague likes to make jokes. I'm going to show you another side of his character. Look at this.' And as though it were the most natural thing in the world, I unbuttoned my blouse, raised my camisole, and bared my breasts. They could all see the bruises that covered them, the welts that never healed. 'If you would like, I could show you the rest. You know your colleague—he does this for laughs...' The three girls stood and, without a word, moved to surround and protect me. The younger of the boys started to cry, and the older one gripped his knife so tightly his knuckles turned white. Our guest also stood and, as calmly as he could manage, moved towards me and said: 'Cover yourself, madame. I understand everything.'

"As for him, he stormed out of the room, pouting like the bad actor he was, slamming the door behind him. I put my clothes back on and began clearing the table. I asked our guest to stay for a while, afraid that the monster would come back in the night and do something criminal. He slept in the living room, right where you're sitting now. We learned the next day that the doctor had gone off somewhere in the night, we didn't know where.

"A few days later, I received a letter from his lawyer informing me that the doctor was in Fredericton and would be staying there for the next few months. I was to return the children to boarding school; he would be selling the house and his practice upon his return. As for me, I could go to hell.

"I did send the kids to school—there was no need for him to ask me to do that—but I stayed in the house, partly because

I had nowhere else to go, and partly because from here I could continue to resist him. He ended up taking an administrative position in Ottawa. He was gone for a year, and when he came back, his health was broken. He never once referred to the incident, and never touched me again. It was as though I had ceased to exist, as though all that unhappiness had been nothing but a long nightmare from which I had finally awakened.

"I sent my daughter to stay with friends in Montreal. She has never set foot in this house again. I see her from time to time, always happily. The other children rarely came back here. They are nothing like their father; they take after their mother. But they were here for his funeral. They're doing well. They know that I love them as if they were my own.

"After that, it became a lot easier to breathe around here. He'd been defeated, and I stayed on. There was no more talk of throwing me out into the street, as he had threatened to do a hundred times before whenever he thought I was questioning his authority.

"But this new turn of events didn't bring me the happiness I'd dreamed of. I had learned to survive during years of unbearable tension, and now that the danger had passed, I felt my strength abandoning me. He never touched me. No more violence, no more sodomy, no more punches. I realized that in all the time I'd been with him, I had never kissed him, and he had never kissed me on the lips. We had never held hands. Suddenly I missed him. Before, he hurt me every time he touched me; now, he hurt me by not touching me. I felt ugly and useless.

"I stopped missing him when I realized he was nothing but a man of straw. The more I looked into his affairs, the more clearly I saw him. He had never been the doctor with a

brilliant future who had chosen to practise in the country out
of pity for the poor and the needy. It's true that he had been
an orphan, that he had fought tooth and nail to go to medical
school, with no other encouragement than the bursaries that
a few philanthropists gave to underprivileged students like
him. But his grades at medical school had been mediocre; he
came to this parish because no one would have him anywhere
else, and no other doctors wanted to come here. The legend
of the dedicated rural doctor was entirely invented by him.
His colleagues laughed at his diagnoses and wrote him off as
a hopeless incompetent. It was lucky for him that the people
in Barachois were more ignorant than he was; they made it
possible for him to play the charitable family physician. Before
long, many of his patients began coming to me to ask about the
medications he'd prescribed for them, and I was able to use my
limited knowledge to avert most of the damage his treatments
would have caused. I helped women during childbirth, and
I gave out medicine from his private dispensary, which had
been his most reliable source of revenue.

"In other words, I became the chatelaine of Wild Caraway.
I protected the doctor from the anger of his patients and colleagues. He wasn't even a good administrator. I had to take
over his books and manage his appointments. I oversaw the
education of his children. He was totally hopeless. He owned a
blueberry farm; I ran that. I ran everything. I was the one who
wore the pants, although I allowed him to bask in the glory
of the good doctor. The poor man was a clown. Look at the
books in the library there behind you. I know for a fact that he
never read a single one of them. He couldn't read music either.
My sister-in-law went to her grave thinking he was a refined

and sophisticated man. All that posing as a man of culture? A joke. The former court jester was never more than a pretender.

"Our feelings follow tortuous paths. You must have found that yourself, have you not? After having been subjugated for so many years, stunned with admiration as I was, martyred in my flesh and in much more intimate places, and stifling all rebellious thoughts because I felt guilty, convinced that I was a person of no value, I became his worst detractor. I hated the love I had once felt for him, and I loved nothing but the hatred and the disgust he inspired in me. It was like that for several years, but in the end it didn't last. I was used to him, and my zeal as his business manager completely cowed him. I began to feel sorry for him. I saw him as a man who had raised himself from an absence of affection by the sheer force of his will, who had abused the generosity of others in order to construct for himself a kingdom of which he was the uncontested master, only to see it collapse under his own weight. He was a tyrant whose abuses drove his subjects to overthrow him, and there was nothing left of him but the shadow of the man whose kingdom had returned to desert, but this time a desert created by his own hand. I reigned over the desert in his stead.

"The last years were almost peaceful. Oh, there were the occasional poisonous eruptions, when nostalgia for the good old days overcame him. If he didn't like a meal I cooked for him, for example, he would throw his plate on the floor like a child having a temper tantrum, and call me an idiot, a fucking asshole, and worse. I would remain calm. 'If you're so unhappy,' I would say to him, 'I can always just let you die, you poor, impotent excuse for a doctor…' Sometimes we'd come to blows, but the next day he would make excuses for his behaviour, and life at Wild Caraway would go on.

"After a while, I no longer thought about our former carnal relationship. He hadn't come to my bedroom for ages. At first I thought little about it; after a while I thought less about it; and finally I didn't think about it at all. I had only one wish, but it would come back every so often: I wanted him to look at me. I put on makeup, I dressed provocatively, I found all kinds of pretexts to put myself in his line of sight, I wore perfume, I smiled. I tricked him into seeing me, and it felt so good, even when he insulted me. I loved it.

"We were stuck with each other, like two shipwrecked sailors on a life raft. Without me, he would have starved to death; without him, so would I. I was all he had; I had no one but him. He was the doctor, I was the housekeeper, and all was right with the world. We each played our role as best we could. There was no applause; we were playing to an empty house.

"Do you know how he spent his final years? Doing what he knew best: play-acting. When he couldn't pretend to be working, he would come out of his sulking convalescence and dress himself up as a different person. You might have seen him tramping through the woods in his Basque beret, the famous botanist in search of medicinal herbs. Or perhaps wearing a straw hat and coveralls, a gentleman farmer who wasn't afraid of getting his hands dirty. Everyone around here fell for it, except him and me. There were even times when we both got into the act: he would dress up in a corduroy jacket and trousers and leaf through a work of great literature without reading it, while I played some air or other on the piano. He loved it when someone dropped in at these moments: we made a perfect *tableau vivant*.

"We would go for drives in the automobile, which was his favourite toy of all. I was the one who drove. The first year he bought it, there were only two vehicles in the area, his and another one owned by the hotel-keeper in Shediac. One day the two drivers passed each other on the road. Neither of them knew how to steer to avoid a collision, and they smashed into each other. The whole parish laughed at that: two cars in the whole region, and they had to run into each other. He never drove after that, he was too afraid. He preferred having a chauffeur, was how he put it. It was fine with me, I loved to drive. So there were some pleasant moments too. Not many.

"Then, bit by bit, we stopped playing our little games, he and I, and went slowly back to behaving like the rest of the world, like friends. There were moments when we could even have talked about a reconciliation. This peace between us lasted just long enough that I felt a tinge of regret when he died."

There was a long pause. She was finished. It was so dark in the room, I could barely see her face. The fire had gone out, and we were both shivering with cold. There was nothing linking us but her melodious voice echoing in the dark. She got up and lit a candle. Then she turned her back to me and her voice became a kind of bleating.

"I've told this story a dozen times already. Telling it makes me feel better, what can I say? Do you remember the two friends who were with me on the beach, digging clams? They can't bear to hear it again. Whenever the three of us got together and had a drop too much to drink, I'd show them my bare breasts and tell them again how I had dethroned the joker-king. The first few times it was all right, they were sympathetic, but after that they didn't want to hear it anymore. So I look around for new audiences. Today I chanced upon you. Do you want to see me naked? No, I can tell you don't. Anyway, I prefer being really drunk when I do my act, and right now the Armagnac has worn off. Another time, perhaps.

"It was good of you to hear me out. You can go now. Good-bye, my dear mime."

Mime. I couldn't believe she had used that word. It had been my nickname in the asylum. How could she possibly have known that? Was it a coincidence? One of those chance connections that love-starved people look for all their lives? No, no more make-believe for me.

I walked home, slowed down by the darkness, trying to recover my peace of mind, like a bad actor who's been booed off the stage. But I didn't dwell too long on my own little misery. After all, my only mistake had been in thinking she might be available. She isn't: she's still in love with this man she waited too long to hate, still living in comfortable captivity, no doubt fearful of any promise of happiness. I understand her; I'm a bit like that myself, sometimes.

Like I said, it's been a bad day.

PART THREE

This morning, the husband asked me to step outside with him so we could talk in private, man to man. In the shade of the apple trees that were looking to give a good crop this year, he told me what I'd been guessing was the case all along. The bank was going to take the house, and his creditors would split the proceeds from the sale of it. Since the property had gained slightly in value since he inherited it, his creditors wouldn't do too badly. They had therefore decided to spare him the humiliation of a public auction, an odious business that is usually held after Mass on Sundays at the home of the bankrupt. Everyone in the parish turns up, and the owners being evicted have to watch the whole thing from start to finish. The bailiff and his henchmen, who have already made an inventory of your possessions, drag everything onto the porch, where your neighbours test the springs of the bed you and your wife made your children in, sift through your things with a little curl of the lip that remains tattooed in your memory forever; your keepsakes are pawed through mercilessly, and you leave your former home with nothing but the clothes on your back and whatever you can cram into a single suitcase, one per person, no more. But the husband tells me they're going to let them leave with whatever they can pack on a horse cart, and he won't have to watch the sale. He figures it's because he's still a man worthy of respect, because he's done everything in his power to avoid bankruptcy. It's more like a surrender than a defeat, he says. He counts himself lucky that he'll be able to start over from square one with some of their furniture, their pots and pans, framed photos of the children. But according to the rules governing bankruptcy, he has to give up all rights to keeping me and receiving the monthly stipend from the parish that has been staving off his ruin for the past few years. Looking down at his feet, he finishes his short speech by saying that soon we'll be parting company and that he'll be sorry to see me go.

I light my pipe and hold out my tobacco pouch to him. I want to keep him talking for a while longer. I'm sure it will do him the world of good, and that by talking about his troubles, sooner or later he'll come up with a thought that will make him feel better.

Sure enough, after talking about this and that for a few minutes, he starts telling me he has a plan, that the future looks fairly rosy. He's an eternal optimist; I'd have been surprised if he'd said anything else. A cranberry farm has just opened near Rogersville, in the north, and they're building a greenhouse next to it. Plenty of jobs opening up, and he knows a foreman who'll take him on, no problem. The future owners will be needing people who can read, and he can do that. He always liked reading when he was a kid, he adds, to convince me and himself. He could even work in an office; he'd be warm in the winter and cool in the summer. He's heard that the pay is all right, too. There might even be work for his oldest boy, who'll be fourteen this fall. "Imagine that! Two paycheques coming in every week! And the little ones, they'll be able to go to a real school with a real teacher who knows lots of real things, with a real blackboard, real chalk to write real words with. Just think! And with the little ones in school, the older girls can stay home and help with the housework, and the wife can get a job at a factory, or find work cleaning houses for rich people. She was in service when she was a young woman, she knows how to handle all that. She's a real trooper, as you well know, sir!" In short, there's a fortune waiting for him up north; here there's nothing but bad luck on land that produces nothing even if you work yourself to death on it every day of the year. The hell with it! He speaks with such conviction about his good fortune that he's bubbling over with joy. I even find myself wanting to believe him.

But his store of good news soon empties. He stops talking, exhausted by his surge of enthusiasm, and the worried expression returns to his face. There's this word in his head that he can't bring himself to say, and so it hangs in the air between us like a storm cloud heavy with hail.

But he has to get it out. "Oh, yes, you... The auction... We'll take care of that... You've had a good few years here, eh? You don't hold this against me, do you?"

I pat him on the shoulder to reassure him. Before going, in order to make sure that I've relieved him of any sense of guilt, I let him know that as far as I'm concerned, the auction is a piece of cake. I'm used to it. I've already been auctioned twice.

"Twice?" he says, holding up two fingers in a V. "But I thought..."

No, no. Twice is right. The first time was when I was just a kid.

I don't know how old I was, maybe seven, maybe nine. No one ever told me what year I was born in; I don't know the month or even the time of year. I know that New Brunswick was still a British colony, but like most people around here, I'm not all that interested in anything that's happened since then.

It was the man I called Papa who brought me to the children's auction. There was a strong wind blowing wet snow, which was why it took us so long to get to Bouctouche from our house on the hill. We went a good part of the way in a buggy driven by Papa's son. Before we left, his daughter-in-law said to me, "Keep your toque on, little guy, we don't want you to catch cold." And turning to Papa, she said, "Come straight back after the sale, don't stop off at the tavern for a couple of beers. I want you back here and alive for dinner."

I didn't have the slightest idea where they were taking me, I just knew that I would never see Papa again, this person I loved and who was the only family I had. His was the only world I had ever known, and to me it was perfect. I was sure that everyone who lived in that house loved each other, even

if they never said it in so many words. They were all good to
me, and I did my best to return their generosity. Those feelings
were enough for me, they were all I needed to grow up happy.

Later, I thought that if a bad family had taken me, Papa
would have brought me home instead of leaving me, and we
would have waited for the next auction sale. Over the years,
that thought was a comfort to me, even though I knew it
wouldn't have been possible because he'd already left the church
when the bidding started; I saw him through the church window, disappearing into the fog. I hung on to the belief anyway
when things were bad; it helped convince me that I hadn't
been abandoned.

The auction took place in the church. The stove smoked, and
the room was as hot as blazes. People in the pews soon had
their hats off and their fur-lined coats unbuttoned. In the
presbytery beside the church, the parishioners had put up a
small counter where people could buy refreshments for a few
cents; the proceeds went into the poor box. Papa and I were
told we could eat for free. A woman with smiling eyes gave me
a plate of buckwheat pancakes with molasses, and a glass of
warm milk that tasted of honey. Papa had sausages and baked
beans, a thick slice of bread, and a cup of tea. I really needed
to go after eating all that, but I didn't dare ask where the toilet
was; in my opinion, it wasn't polite to use the toilet in a priest's
house, especially right after they fed you. So I held it in, and
because it was so hot, I fell asleep and the urge went away.

I had to have a medical. I remember a nurse taking off
my shirt, a doctor asking me to cough and listening to my
heart. I was blushing because no stranger had ever touched

me before, only my mother and Nanna, and that had been
a long time ago. The doctor and nurse asked Papa a pile of
questions. What they were most interested in was my refusal
to speak. They considered it a kind of illness. He told them
not to pay too much attention to it. "He's intelligent, in his
own way, and he understands everything that's said to him,
even complicated things. You just have to get used to him."
I remember Papa asking if my being dumb would lower my
price, and they said there was no way to tell.

Then the government inspector came in. He was a small
man, but stocky, and with a loud voice that somehow softened,
like magic, when he spoke to me. I liked him right away; he
seemed to be someone who would protect children against
ugly, evil grown-ups. I also liked what he was wearing. He was
distinguished-looking in his wide-brimmed felt hat and his
long greatcoat. He walked with a cane and had a gold watch
in the pocket of his waistcoat. He took it out every couple of
minutes to check the time. He saw me being interested in the
watch, and it evidently pleased him. "You don't talk much, do
you, boy?" he said. "But you seem pretty smart to me. Look
at my watch. I'm going to say a certain time, and if it's not
the right time, I want you to do nothing. But if I say the right
time, you nod your head. Okay?" I loved this game — it was
easy as pie and I had an audience watching me. The nurse and
the doctor paid close attention. The inspector said it was noon,
two-thirty, five after ten, and so on, and after eleven times I
nodded my head: it was twenty past one. He put his watch
back in his pocket like a man who was satisfied with his own
performance. "I told you he was smart," he said. The nurse
and doctor nodded. I suddenly felt happy and confident again.

The inspector said he had to go because he had another appointment, but before he left, he gave me a stick of hard toffee wrapped in red and gold paper that had a picture of a pretty blond girl on it wearing a beret with a feather and some ribbons hanging from one side of it. I felt rich, holding that stick of candy in my hand like a promise of pleasure and happiness. It made me feel respected, appreciated. After all, I'd earned it by being smart.

Then the inspector sat in a corner and had a quiet conversation with Papa. I was in the opposite corner, between the nurse and the doctor. The doctor talked while the nurse wrote things down and I looked at the doctor's instruments. I could hear everything he said, but there were a lot of words I didn't know. It didn't bother me, though, because none of them sounded threatening, and the nurse's face stayed calm. No need to worry, then. I fell asleep again.

When the inspector and Papa were finished, we were led out of the manse. There were a lot of people in the hallway, standing about and talking, and children with long faces lined up against one wall. I didn't know it, but they were going to be auctioned off too. None of us knew what to expect, we didn't even know we'd be competing with each other for the best families. We just stood and stared at each other. Then Papa and I were told to go into the church and sit up in the choir loft. The altar had been taken down for the occasion, and a large curtain drawn in front of the crucifix so no one could see it. It was the first time I'd ever been in a church. I liked the smell of burning incense, a fondness that has stayed with me. The first time I saw the woman I loved was in a church, and there was the smell of incense there too, and I remember thinking at the time that it was a good sign, good enough to erase the memory of the children's auction.

I was content to be alone again with Papa. He didn't say anything, but from time to time he put his arm around my shoulder and pulled me close to him, or sometimes he took my hand and then let it go. A woman in a grey uniform came and sat beside us. She was from the orphanage; a lot of the children being auctioned came from there. She told us in a friendly tone of voice that there were twenty minutes to go. In an even kinder voice, she told me that Papa would have to sit in the general audience, and that I'd be able to say goodbye to him later. She didn't add, "for the last time." A few moments later, Papa gave me a pat on the knee and said, "I have to go. Be a good boy. I'm proud of you. Everything will turn out for the best, you'll see." I hardly knew what to think. He stood up and walked straight towards the big door at the back. I followed his green woollen toque as it went out through the crowd that was coming in. I saw him open the big door and leave.

I've replayed that scene in my head any number of times, and each time it's a little different. I've imagined his cheeks running with tears, his voice breaking under the pressure of his emotions, or him stopping at the door, turning, and running back to hug me for the first and last time. I've pictured him arguing with the government inspector, suddenly becoming angry, telling him he'd changed his mind and was taking me back home. Nothing like that happened, of course. My favourite version is also the most absurd: Papa sitting in the audience and bidding for me, outbidding everyone else so that he could take me home again. Obviously that didn't happen, but it gave me a great deal of pleasure thinking about it.

The other children came one by one to sit with me in the choir, with each one being introduced by the woman in the grey uniform. I still remember their names: there was Francis, Paul, two Pierres, Laetitia and Mai, who were twins, two Margarets, one who called herself Peggy and the other Maggy, Egmont, Napoleon, Bartholomew... Each time she said my name, she explained that I didn't know how to talk, which wasn't exactly true, but I didn't bother setting her straight. A few of my new comrades seemed ashamed to be there, and kept their heads down. Maybe they had been there before and knew what was going to happen. People were coming into the church and it was filling up quickly, the murmur of the crowd growing louder and, for some reason, jollier, as if this was some kind of holiday. I noticed that some of the men were taking nips of alcohol from flasks they kept hidden in their coats, and that they were the ones who were talking loudest.

My only disappointment came when I noticed that some of the other children were holding sticks of toffee like the one the inspector had given me; a few were even waving them around, not even looking at them. Had they passed the watch test too? Suddenly I didn't feel so special, I felt like all the others, no longer so intelligent and unique. I looked at my companions to see if any of them didn't have a toffee stick, because I wanted to give mine away so I would feel powerful and good, like the inspector. I thought I could pass my pleasure on to them, and understand what it was like to be normal. I noticed a girl of about my age who was wearing a grey uniform like that of the woman. I held out my toffee stick to her, but she whispered that she already had one, and she opened her little bag and showed it to me, but she did it without making a sound, as though her having the toffee was against the rules. She didn't take mine. Maybe she thought that having two would be unfair; or perhaps she thought I wasn't important enough to be allowed to feel generous towards my equals. Her refusal didn't hurt me, it made me feel ordinary again.

Then the bailiff came in, shaking people's hands and carrying a big pile of papers. He looked important and well-liked. He put the papers on the lectern and his glasses on his nose, and the crowd gave a little cough when he cleared his throat and said: "Ladies and gentlemen, I declare the auction open…" There were thirteen children to place. First up were the two twins. Everything went so slowly that I began to feel sleepy again, and I had to resist with all my strength a desire to nod off, because it wouldn't look good if I appeared so indifferent to my fate that I couldn't even stay awake for it.

My turn came. "Ladies and gentlemen," said the bailiff, "this boy may not be a rare gem, but he is certainly worth a close look. He's as smart as a monkey, as agile as a cat, and as healthy as a horse. He's been well fed, coming from a family that has always cared for its children. It isn't misfortune that has landed him here. It's simply that he no longer has a mother, or a father, really, and the man who was looking after him is too old to keep him anymore. The only mark against him is that he doesn't talk; he wouldn't say boo if his life depended on it. Now mind, this could be a good thing. For example, you won't hear him complaining. But don't get me wrong: he understands everything that's said to him. You don't have to shout at him, either. He's compliant and isn't afraid of work. You won't have to make him take care of himself; he keeps himself clean and doesn't wet the bed at night." I was happy when he finished, because I was beginning to be embarrassed. Someone in the audience stood up to get a better look at me — a woman who had put on her glasses. I smiled at her automatically.

I got the feeling that people were looking at me with special interest, and I returned their gaze to show them I wasn't afraid. For a brief moment I even thought I should behave as though I were the one choosing a family, not the other way around, but I knew that wasn't the case, and so I gave it up.

Someone in the choir started to cry. It was one of the twins, who was wailing at the idea of being separated from her sister, and before long most of the others were snivelling or sobbing too. A small blond boy screamed as if the world were coming to an end. I didn't cry, but it wasn't because I was braver than the others. I was the same as everyone else, but when I cried, it was only in my head. When I'm suffering, all the bones in my face hurt, and if anyone looks at me, I lower my eyes.

The crowd was sympathetic to all the crying, but the bailiff went on with his work. He kept a cool head and did his job. In the end, the twins were separated. One went for a good price while the other, the one who cried, went for almost nothing. Everyone seemed to feel sorry for her. People always pitied children who were sent to the auction, and they felt extra sorry for those who weren't taken and had to go to the orphanage. The children who cried hardest were those who'd already been to the orphanage and now had to go back. They thought they'd had a chance to live with a family, out in the real world, and now they had to face the fact that no one wanted them. They were the ones most likely to run away, and the orphanage employees, such as the woman in the grey uniform, kept a close eye on them. Because if it was a day like this one, with a full storm raging outside, they would surely freeze or starve to death if they ran away, and their bodies would be eaten by foxes or coyotes. That was why they always had their warm clothes taken away the moment they got there, to remove all temptation, and it was also why they were sometimes given a drug to make them sleepy.

I'd never set foot in an orphanage, but I'd heard horrible things about them: that the children were mistreated, starved, beaten, made to work until they dropped. The children fought amongst themselves, too, and some of them hanged themselves out of despair. I believed these stories, not because I thought they were true but because I didn't want to take any chances. In fact, I'd heard them before I was even born; they were told to my mother by people who were worried about the child she was carrying, who was me. I heard them again later, after I was born, from people who thought the stories would make me behave. The day I was auctioned, I was afraid for a while that I wouldn't be taken and would go to the orphanage with the woman in grey, and that was why I went into it already inclined to be grateful to the family that was going to be so kind as take me home with them.

I went for four dollars, which wasn't bad considering I'd started at six. If you go for a good price, you enter a kind of aristocracy. A glorious halo surrounds you. No one knows exactly why you go for what you do—maybe because you look sturdy and reliable, or because there's a shortage of workers in a particular area. Your physique might have something to do with it too. All anyone knows is how long the auction took and how much they were willing to let you go for. You don't try to figure out why you were popular that day; all that matters is that you were taken. I went for a middling amount, and my auction lasted less than fifteen minutes.

Papa would have liked the family that took me. The man seemed all right; he had bright eyes and a soft voice. The moment I saw him, I knew that things would go well at his house if I kept my head down. He also took the little blond boy, the one who cried his lungs out. He went for two dollars, which gave me a certain advantage over him. I think he always resented me for it, especially after we found out that he was older than me. It didn't mean a thing to me, except that I did find his resentment a bit flattering.

When the day was over, the bailiff and the man signed some papers. The man knew how to read and write — another good sign, I told myself. No one in my family had been able to do that except my aunt, and even she only read picture books, and always the same ones. Only two children were sent to the orphanage. All the same, I felt sorry for them.

The man told us to get our things and follow him. He asked if we were hungry or thirsty, or if we needed to go to the toilet, because we were going to spend the next three hours in a buggy. Neither of us said anything. "When you address me,"

he said before we left, "you call me Sir, do you understand?"
He didn't need to tell us twice.

I slept for the whole trip. It was dark when we got there.
For years I thought we'd travelled a long way, at least a long
way from where Nanna and Papa lived. But it was only up to
Cap-Lumière, about a day's walk from my first family.

(The only time I saw my old house again, there were strangers living in it, people who had come from somewhere far
away. But I was the stranger in their house. I didn't even
understand their language. The house had been repainted.
The well was still in the same place, of course, and the apple
trees were in good shape. The old chicken shed, where I'd been
born, had been torn down. I didn't ask what had happened
to the house's former occupants; I was afraid of finding out
that Papa had gone to the auction too. I left as soon as I could
decently get away.)

When the blond boy and I went into Sir's house, the family
had already had supper and the table had been cleared. The
woman took our coats and told us to sit in the kitchen, where
she served us a *fricot* with bread that was still warm from
the oven. Our arrival had caused a bit of a stir in the house,
and the other children were sitting around the kitchen table,
watching us. It made me so nervous I could barely eat, my
hands were shaking so much. I never liked people watching
me, and there I was the centre of attention, along with Sir and
the blond boy. Luckily, the blond boy liked being looked at,
and he started talking a blue streak. The girls thought he was
as cute as a button and weren't shy about saying so; he seemed
to have endeared himself to them with his babbling. As for

me, it looked as though I was to be the object of the boys' attention. I felt a certain satisfaction when the man told the blond boy to pipe down and eat his supper if he didn't have anything interesting to say. The boy's eyes filled with tears, and one of the girls smoothed his hair to let him know that everything was all right. Lucky guy.

All told, there were four boys and three girls, all older than us. After a few minutes, while we were still eating our fricot, the boys pretended to become interested in something else and began talking loudly and laughing, but I could tell they were still keeping a wary eye on us. The girls watched us more openly, and talked about us as if we weren't there. It didn't take them long to make up their minds that the blond boy was the cuter of the two—which I admit was true—and that he would be their favourite—which made me feel bad. They also decided that he would sleep in their bedroom and I would bunk in with the boys. I would have given everything I had to switch places with him, but I didn't have anything, and so I acted as though I hadn't heard them.

The mother also had a kind face, like her husband, but she didn't seem to be the sort who could be taken in easily; my first thought was that I would have my work cut out for me getting into her good graces. I would have to be patient, and even then she might not like me. "Why did you get two?" she said to the father. "One would have been enough. The blond boy, for example, for the girls to play with." I later learned that one of the sons had almost died of swamp fever the year before, and the mother had made a vow to take in an orphan if her son got better. The father told her he bid on me first because they said I was healthy, and one day they'd need someone to work on the farm when their oldest boy went off on his own. And he took the blond boy because he didn't want me to be alone, and also because he looked as if he was in need of a good family. The blond boy would be the fulfillment of the mother's vow; I would be the future farm labourer.

"How long will they be here," asked a small, grave voice, "and can we send them back if we don't like them?" The voice belonged to the palest of the boys, who I thought for a long time had been the sick one who had inspired the mother's vow. Of all the boys, he was the least happy about our being there. But I was wrong, it was another boy who'd been sick.

All the father said was that we wouldn't be staying there at all if the family didn't pass the government inspection. An agent would be coming by in the spring or early summer to see if we were being well treated, and if we passed inspection, we would stay there until we were at least sixteen years old — or twenty-one, if the agent thought we were incapable of looking after ourselves.

"Will they have the same last name as us?" asked another boy.

"No," said the mother, a little too quickly, I thought.

"How old is he?" asked one of the girls, pointing at me. Her voice in the half-light made me blush.

"I don't know," said the father. "He doesn't know either. It isn't his fault. We'll ask the doctor when he comes. The other one has a birth certificate."

The father gave a sign that said the conversation was over. They all looked at me for a while as if I had done something. Again, I pretended I hadn't understood what they were talking about, something I've been doing almost my entire life.

Sir finished his meal, and when he stood up, so did everyone else. He was the master of the house, no doubt about that. Out of habit, I did what I had always done in my previous house: I took my glass, utensils, and plate over to the sink and began to wash them. One of the boys gave a loud snort, which he wanted me to hear.

"Just leave them on the counter," said the mother. "Here, it's the girls who clear the table and do the dishes. No one else."

It was my first faux pas, but not my last.

When it was time to go upstairs to bed, I followed the boys to their room. They weren't exactly happy to have me, but they seemed less hostile than before, although still a bit annoyed at having to share their room with an outsider. They set me up in a corner where my things had been deposited, beside a mattress and close to the chamber pot. That first night I barely slept, afraid that one of the boys would get up to relieve himself and I would be splattered with piss.

There was another thing that bothered me even more. In the next room, the girls were playing with their new Little Prince, and it was torture for me to have to listen to them. I was so jealous, I would have cried if I could. They swooned around him, stroked his hair, praised his good looks, exclaimed over the sweetness of his voice. He was their little doll. The only time they complained was when they wanted to wash him and the mother came in and told them to calm down, that she and she alone would get him ready for bed that night. I fell asleep listening to their happy giggles, feeling jealous and miserable. I was alone in a corner with a piss pot beside my bed, and he was sharing his bed with one of the girls. Which one? I tried to guess, if only to make myself feel worse, and to get used to feeling worse until the day came when I would no longer feel anything.

The oldest boy woke me in the morning. We had to get dressed, go downstairs, and slip out of the house without making any noise, then help the father in the barn and look after the chickens. Someday, the boy whispered, we would be doing this on our own, while the father slept in. He showed me where I could relieve myself, on the manure pile beside the barn. "I hope you ain't afraid of rats," he said. He didn't tell me his name, and it took me a long time to figure out what everyone was called. No one bothered to introduce themselves to me. They all existed in my head, but I hardly figured at all in theirs. I was their little hireling, which is what they called me after that, even when I had become a man.

The first days were hard, because of my undeclared rivalry with the little blond boy, a contest he won hands down day after day. He never had to do a thing around the house except play with the girls. I was especially jealous of him when the girls argued over whose turn it was to bathe him, and they took a long time doing it. They never tired of finding new qualities to marvel at: how soft his skin was, how blond the hairs on his arm, how white his teeth, how curly his hair, how violet his eyes. The long and the short of it was, he had everything going for him, the master of the universe I dreamed of entering. Sometimes I even thought he was lucky to have been orphaned.

Not only was he as cute as a button, he was also a genuine orphan, not just a kid found by the side of the road or on the church steps on Easter Sunday. He'd had real parents, whose names he knew. His mother had died of pneumonia while he was in the room with her, and his father, who was a deep-sea fisherman, had drowned nobly at sea. The girls' estimation of him increased a hundredfold every day. He was frail, too, and the girls loved playing hospital with him, and smothering him with tender kisses whenever he was sick. They literally fought with each other over the right to look after him. Their tussles became so ferocious, they ended up having to make a list of whose turn it was and follow it. Naturally, the boys never fought over the honour of watching me take a piss, and the blond boy's luck made me grind my teeth with envy. What was more, I never got sick, so I didn't stand a chance against him.

There was only one thing that dampened their enthusiasm for him. One morning I heard a cry of alarm coming from their bedroom. The boy had pissed the bed, and the girl whose bed he'd been in that night was soaked to the skin. I felt so good when I heard it that I felt bad. The girls did everything they could to hide the accident from their mother. They washed him, kept their voices down when they scolded him, made him promise not to do it again, and washed the sheets on the sly. The boys came over to see if I'd done the same thing, but the straw in my mattress was dry. The eldest of them said to the girls, "Yours might be easier to look at, but at least ours is toilet trained." I had won my first victory over my seductive rival.

A few nights later, he did it again, and before long he was wetting his bed every night. Suddenly the girls weren't so eager to sleep with him, and there was no more fighting over that particular honour. When the mother found out about his pissing himself, she whipped him out of the girls' room and exiled him to ours. The girls didn't protest too much; there was something about what had happened that hinted at an act of nature they didn't want to know too much about. I heard the youngest one asking the others: "Does Daddy peepee on Mommy? It must be awful to live with a man who does that to you every night." Finally there was a chink in the little blond boy's armour.

It would have been a real victory if the little blond boy had been relegated to the boys' room and I had been moved into the girls' room to take his place, but there was no danger of that. When the eldest went off to college, they removed his bed to make more space for my mattress. My rival was assigned to sleep on my mattress, with me, and he pissed himself at least once a week for the next three months.

The other boys hated him for filling their bedroom with the smell of urine. One day, after breakfast, when the parents and girls were off somewhere, they dragged him into the yard and held him upside down by his feet over the well, saying they would drop him down it if he didn't stop pissing his bed at night. The kid cried for two days; even I was shocked by what they'd done. The girls were horrified when they found out what had happened to their former pet, and he became even more their darling than he had been before. That made me more disgusted with the boys' behaviour than I already was: their cruelty had transformed him from the guilty party into the victim, another battle gone to him even though he'd done nothing to deserve the win. But he'd already suffered enough, so there wasn't much I could do about it.

In any case, he stopped pissing himself. That, at least, was something.

Those first days in the house, I thought I would die of boredom. I missed Papa and Nanna. Every time I thought about them, I tried as hard as I could to think of something else, but no dice. To some extent, their memory haunted me less when I finally accepted my situation and began to enjoy my new home. I missed my half-sister and my aunt too, but that hollow feeling slowly diminished as well. They remain part of my life, they haven't faded from my memory at all; I can still call up images of myself with them, as a child. Papa and Nanna will always live in my head, him smoking raw tobacco in his crooked pipe and her sitting with him beside the stove, darning socks and telling sad stories to pass the time. My aunt in her wheelchair, my half-sister sitting at her little table, drawing, while I play in a corner with my toy soldiers, all of which have been decapitated at least once, and whose heads I have patiently glued back onto their leaden bodies.

There wasn't a lot of joy with my new family, but farm work at least saved me from being bored. The little agriculture we practised provided cheap food for the table: vegetables from the garden, fruit from the orchard, milk and cheese from the goats and cows. We also raised pigs and chickens. The father's main source of income was the general store he ran in the village. He was also the parish clerk, a position that added to his revenue and, more importantly, increased his social status. Few decisions were made in the district without him; his opinions carried weight. His wife had been a teacher when she was young, and that also added to the family's prestige.

The boys and girls all had chores on the farm, but their duties were more about teaching them how to get on in life. Certain virtues were imparted through them: the value of a job well done, a sense of responsibility, and so on. The bulk of the work was left to the little hireling, and since I was the new hired hand, that meant me. I didn't mind: I was earning a living, and in any case Papa had taught me how to do a lot of things. I would have been his helper if he'd kept me with him.

Everything I was doing here was a continuation of my old life. My path seemed to have been set out for the next several years: I would grow up and one day I would leave. Until then, I had to spend my time usefully. Since I was deemed to be "a little special," that was the only life there was for me in that place.

But then something happened to change my small, sad universe. I soon got used to the work on the farm, and I liked hearing Sir say to his wife: "He's a good worker, always ready to walk that extra mile. I think we should keep him. In fact, given the price I paid for him, he's a bargain." He might have added: "But I'm not so sure of the girls' little blond poppet," but he never said that. The little blond poppet was part of the family. They even talked about adopting him one day. He went to school with the other boys during the week, and he went to church with the family on Sundays, where he sat in the pew with the girls, who were happy showing off their pet.

But all in all, things were going pretty well. The boys kept their distance—I was, after all, just a hireling—but they were friendly enough and grateful that I could take over some of their duties on the farm. As for the girls, when occasionally they tired of playing with the blond kid, they would turn their maternal attentions on me. They didn't exactly flood me with idle affections, but they did show some interest in me and tried to be nice enough. I didn't lower my guard, or go out of my way to attract attention to myself, but I was always eager to run errands for them, and I believe they appreciated the fact that I knew my place in the household. But even for them I was never more than the little hireling, not a child like them or the little blond kid. But that was all right by me, and no one gave me any grief. Only the mother scared me, because I was sure she could read my mind.

The turning point came in the form of a game of checkers. In my former house, Nanna had been a kind of regional checkers champion, and she had taught me how to play. My new family took out the checkerboard and the pieces from time to time, on Sundays or when it rained. No one ever invited me to play, of course, but they let me watch.

Someone noticed my interest, but the first time one of the boys asked me if I wanted to play, the others all laughed, and I backed off, keeping my head down. The father scolded them in a gruff voice. "Look, he can't talk, he can't play, he's not like other boys, as you well know. He can work hard, but play? I don't think so. Leave him alone, don't ask him to join in." I bit my lip, telling myself I'd been smart to shy away: the time wasn't ripe.

One Saturday during my second winter with them—I must have been about eleven—the middle sister got out the game, but no one wanted to play with her. Suddenly she looked up and asked her mother if she could teach me to play. "You can try," her mother said. The girl told me to sit across from her. I was going to play black, she explained, and she would be red. Then she went through the rules in such great detail I thought she would never end. It was almost suppertime, we would have to eat, and the game would be postponed indefinitely, and I was dying to play. I feigned as much interest as I could in order to speed her up. I let her win the first game to show that I was an eager beginner. She complimented me on my progress. "You see? It's not that difficult, is it?" I let the second game go on for a while, and with my help she won that one too. She complimented me again. "See, Mother, he can learn after all.

He may be dumb, but he's not stupid. Come on, let's play one more game before supper." I didn't let her off so easy this time: I beat her before she even realized what had happened. She sat there with her mouth hanging open, then looked around to see if anyone had been watching. Luckily for her, the others were busy at the table. She looked at me for a moment without saying anything; I looked back as if I didn't know what I had done. For a moment I was afraid she would be angry and put the game away, but she was far too smart for that.

She put a finger to her lips to tell me to keep quiet about my victory, and signalled me to follow her to the dinner table. When we were sitting down, she said, "I've just taught the little hireling how to play checkers. He is capable of learning. He even has a knack for it, I think. I'm tired now, but if any of you want to play with him after supper, you'll see..." One of the boys told her he didn't believe her. The two other girls laughed, but not maliciously.

After supper, my checkers teacher challenged everyone to play against me. I knew what she was doing: I was her champion, proof positive of her skill as a teacher. I was happy to repay her for having shown a bit of interest in me. After some prodding, the oldest daughter agreed to play, but only one game. I beat her in two minutes flat. My teacher was ecstatic. "You see? When you take your time with slow children, you can teach them anything. Even a little farm boy." She was obviously more impressed with her own ability to teach than with my ability to learn. She never played me again, and seemed happy that I didn't speak and therefore couldn't tell anyone that I had beaten her too. Naturally, I kept her secret, and she let me know she was grateful for that.

"Anyone else want to play him?" she asked.

The eldest boy said he would, but I think only to shut her up. In the end I played them all, and beat them one after the other. After that, no one wanted to play me, and no one said a word. Had I perhaps gone too far?

It wasn't winning that gave me the most pleasure, even though it did stop them from treating me like a moron; it was the fact that for a brief moment the spotlight had been taken off the little blond boy. He was too clever to play against me, but I had gained an advantage over him: my teacher was no longer constantly occupied with him, it was as though a distancing had occurred, something from which I might be able to benefit later on. Amazed by her triumph, she had suddenly acquired a subject with whom she could play school and do good, and advance her vocation as a schoolteacher at the same time. Could I perhaps become her creation, her own Little Prince? My secret victory made me greedy and sneaky. I told myself that if I could win the hearts of the two other daughters as I had won that of their sister, thanks to the game of checkers, the three of them would abandon their blond poppet and, who knew, maybe want to give me my bath and let me sleep in their beds at night. (At least I wouldn't pee on them.) But I knew right away that such dreams were dangerous; that place in their hearts was already taken, the idea they had of me was fixed and immutable. We lived in an order that couldn't be challenged. I realized it in time and avoided making that mistake.

There was, however, a tradition in the family that helped advance my cause. They organized checkers tournaments on holidays, and whoever won had the right to play against the mother, who was an excellent player and never lost. To play against her was a coveted honour. After I won the first tournament I took part in, my teacher asked her if she would like to play a game with me. The mother, looking at me severely, replied: "He's beaten all of you. He's not a bad player, but he probably knew how to play long before he ever set foot in this house." I lowered my gaze and, for a moment, to punish her for having twigged to my little game, imagined her giving me my bath and bringing me into her bed. I quickly chased such forbidden thoughts from my mind, since they could hardly serve my purpose. Luckily, the father drew attention to himself by declaring that he would play a game against me. Everyone gathered around us. It took me a while, but I let him win. Everyone clapped except the mother, who was not fooled by my diplomatic loss. But all the same, I had returned things to their natural state, I hadn't overstepped my position, order had been restored.

Another time, after I had beaten everyone, including the father, the mother agreed to play the new house champion. I remember her looking straight into my eyes, as if to say she wasn't taken in by me the way the others were. I dropped all pretence of being a talented novice and did my best to beat her. I saw right away that she was very good; I won only one game out of three. We never played again after that, but the fact that I'd dealt honestly with her put her in a better frame of mind towards me.

The least that can be said about my skill at checkers is that it improved my status in the family. Sir spoke more kindly to me after that, as if my prowess had changed me into a normal human being. The boys stopped taking me for a simpleton, and kept their cruel comments to themselves. With the girls, however, I had scored a real victory. I had proven to them that I was good for something other than feeding chickens and forking manure.

People feel good about themselves when they teach you something; they think they have improved themselves, and you have been improved in their eyes. Their estimation of you rises to the same level as their estimation of themselves. They have raised you to their height, and they treat you like a creature they themselves have created in their image. Thus they have a higher opinion of themselves, and in their moments of generosity a little of their love of themselves rubs off on you. You should never pass up an opportunity to be improved. It pays dividends.

But it meant I had a teacher on my back. She thought of nothing but how she could realize her ambition through me, and she was too full of herself to see me as clearly as her mother did. She saw herself through my eyes, and what she saw was beauty and intelligence, never mind that what I saw was the opposite. In any case, she never left me alone after that, and her selfish interest had its good as well as its bad side.

On the good side, she decided that, given her genius as a teacher, she would get me reading and writing, as well as doing arithmetic, music, and geography. Most of all, she would teach me to speak. That was the worst part. I couldn't explain to her why I'd taken a vow of silence, and she was convinced that my not talking was a minor flaw that she could correct with determination and skill—hers. I resisted as much as I could, while pretending to be interested. Each time she made me repeat a word or a letter, I would hold my breath as long as I could, puffing out my cheeks and letting my face turn red.

That discouraged her, but I think it was her fear of failure that made her give up. I knew my ordeal was over when I heard her say: "I think this is a bit hard for you. We'll try again later." She ended up postponing her diction lessons so often that eventually she stopped mentioning them altogether. But to stay in her good graces, I let her teach me to play the piano and a few card games. I already knew how to play the piano by ear, and there wasn't a card game on earth I didn't know, thanks to Nanny and Papa. All I had to do was show slow but steady improvement, never getting too far ahead of myself. She was as eager as a kitten at the beginning of each lesson, but as soon as the teaching became too difficult for her liking, she dropped me like a doll she'd grown tired of playing with. I found it hard, being treated like that, and secretly wished she would leave me alone. But at least through her I learned a little of what it was like to go to school.

On the bad side, there were the piano lessons. She could read music tolerably well, and compared with the others she could easily pass for a talented player. But she couldn't even tell that the piano was out of tune. In this case, pretending ignorance and yet showing an interest required more effort. Luckily, her lousy playing produced so many complaints from the others that she soon moved on to my geography lessons, using the huge globe that she had as a teaching aid. But I liked music. One Sunday, when the family was at church, I sat down at the piano and played some of my favourite songs, but I was careful never to show her that I knew more than she did.

The first time I played a sonatina from beginning to end, in front of the assembled family, my teacher applauded warmly. Even the little blond boy clapped his hands. What no one knew was that I was playing to the sister I liked best, the youngest one. I remember looking at her longer than usual to see if she was aware of my feelings towards her, but it was a waste of time. The first time we love, we love alone. It takes time for love to be reciprocated. Fortunately, it always is, sooner or later, especially if you have loved alone for a long time.

I know now why I found the youngest daughter so appealing: no one else in the household paid much attention to her. She hardly existed in their eyes, which made her kind of my companion in misfortune. There was also the fact that the middle sister made her read stories to me out loud. She had a book of tales, covered in leather, that I found very beautiful. She loved to read to me in the evenings, and these tales enchanted me. There were times when I was sure that they'd been written just for me. I especially liked the ones in which wandering young boys ended up slaying giants and stealing their treasure, but the one I liked best of all was about a young girl who used her long hair to let her lover climb up to the prison where she was being kept. That one made me dream more than the others, and for years I believed it was a true story.

Whenever she opened her book and asked me to sit beside her on the sofa, my heart began to beat faster, and before I knew it I was in love with her and her world of words and pictures. But I ceased to exist for her the moment she closed the book, and she left without even bidding me good night. In her eyes too, I was nothing but a lifeless toy that she could play with when she felt like it. That was why I stopped loving her.

All this thirst for knowledge at least had the effect of pushing the little blond boy out of the limelight. My rival didn't suspect a thing. The two other girls tried to imitate their teacher sister with him, but they quickly discovered that nothing interested him. At school he never paid attention, he had trouble spelling his own name, and that didn't sit well with the mother, who was a former teacher. I secretly relished his frequent disappointments in that area, and it ticked me off that his shortcomings never seemed to bother him at all. He was still the Master of the Daughters because he was cute; unlike me, he hadn't had to acquire political awareness. But as a rule, he was no longer a threat to me.

His popularity finally dropped to zero the day the doctor came to see us, about eighteen months after we got there. We were both examined, and the doctor told everyone that the little blond boy was at least two years older than me. That day the mother decreed that he would no longer take his baths with the girls. And she yanked him out of school too, so he could learn a trade.

All things considered, life was good. At least it wasn't the orphanage, and my situation was almost enjoyable. I had my place, I was their little hireling, and I was on good terms with all of them. I never became friends with the little blond boy, but we managed to get along fairly well.

The house was almost empty by the time I left. My little teacher had gone to the convent, and then on to normal school. After she graduated, she taught for a while, got married, and ended up living in Fredericton. I can't say I missed her.

The eldest sister became a nun. She was kind enough to leave her most precious possession behind: the globe with which her sister had taught me geography and the bit of history she knew. I liked touching it when I went over my lessons. I still know the names of all the countries of the world and their capitals, what the people who live in them are called, and the languages they speak.

As for the youngest, the least loved of the family, the one I liked most, she went off to look after a distant relative and I never heard from her again.

The sick brother to whom the little blond boy owed his presence in the family drowned three years after our arrival. He'd always been unlucky. His absence cast a dark shadow on our lives. The mother died the next year, as bitter and broken-hearted as a jilted lover. I didn't think it would be, but her death was painful to me, and I carry the memory of it to this day like an unhealed wound. I'd always dreamed of winning her over, and it never happened. Maybe because I wasn't clever or likeable enough, I'll never know. In any case, her memory has never left me.

The cute little blond kid, who remained cute and blond and little, was apprenticed to a butcher in the next parish, and we never saw him again either. We had almost become friends after the last sister left home and there was no one left to feed my stupid rivalry with him.

That left Sir, who sold his general store to an outsider, and the eldest son, who had gone off to study agronomy. He would inherit the farm one day, which had undergone many expansions. He had married and already had two daughters. I got along well with his wife, but she didn't exactly cozy up to me in any big way. As far as she was concerned, I was the odd one out in the household, which didn't surprise me much because I was the odd one out in my own eyes too.

One day, a government agent stopped by to see how I was doing. "I don't know what age your hired hand is, to be honest," he said to Sir, "but he looks to me to be older than sixteen. Now that he's able to earn his living on his own, I'll have to let him go. If you want to keep him on, you'll have to pay him like you would any other employee, otherwise you'd be exploiting a ward of the province. That would be at least twenty dollars a month, less what it costs you for his bed and board. Or you can let him find work somewhere else. If he decides to leave, you can't stop him. There's a third possibility: if you adopt him officially, he will have to stay here until he's twenty-one, and his work won't cost you a cent. I'll need a response before the end of the year. I'll come back before winter, so think it over and let me know what you plan on doing."

Sir said he'd give it some thought. I was standing behind him the whole time he was talking to the agent, terrified that he was going to adopt me on the spot. I didn't want to be given his name, I didn't want to have any name, I just wanted to be free. Lucky for me that his son and his son's wife would never let me become a member of the family; they wouldn't want to have to share their inheritance with a stranger. Their greed was my passport to freedom.

The next morning, after chores, I dressed in clothes that had been left behind by the other boys because they didn't want them, and I packed my rucksack. I had my hat on my head and I was ready to go. I didn't have a red cent to my name, all I owned was myself, and I felt like the most liberated man on earth, which gave me a blast of courage. Sir wasn't pleased. "So, you're leaving? Just like that? You could have given me some warning, at least. It would have been the polite thing to do." But we both knew that for once I had the law on my side, and he couldn't keep me against my will. I didn't want to be simply tolerated in this house in exchange for my work. He would have done the same if he'd been me. I'd finished the morning chores, so I wouldn't leave him high and dry.

With a sigh, he took the roll of bills he always carried from his pocket and began counting out a few dollars. I shook my head; he didn't owe me anything. I could have used the money, since I didn't have any, but I was too happy being able to rob him of the opportunity to be the big shot in his own eyes. My refusal seemed to pain him a bit, and I sensed him hesitating between being affronted and being relieved. He quietly slipped the roll back into his pocket when his daughter-in-law came out of the house to join us. I grinned at him. It was the first time I'd ever seen him be afraid of a family member. I thought: "Times are changing. Sir is not the only master in the house anymore. It's a good time to move on."

The daughter-in-law didn't accuse me of anything, but she asked me to open my rucksack to make sure I hadn't taken anything that didn't belong to me — by mistake, she said. By mistake...She was a piece of work, that one. She also made me take off my coat so she could check my pockets, and I handed it over to her gladly, because I knew there was nothing in them. Sir turned away as if he was ashamed. I picked up my pack, turned my back on them, and left. The two little girls came down from the porch to say goodbye, and I returned their waves for no better reason than to annoy the daughter-in-law. The son was in the field harnessing the mare. He didn't wave, just went about his work as though nothing was happening, probably because he too was afraid of his wife.

That day, nothing existed except me and the road ahead. I was so happy, I didn't feel the stinging cold rain in my face. From now on, no one would be able to order me around; as of today, they would have to ask me politely and thank me afterwards. I walked for about an hour, then sat on a stump beside the road because I felt like crying. It had stopped raining, I was a bit hungry, I was soaked to the skin, but my wet skin was that of a free man. Despite the daughter-in-law's behaviour at the end, I hadn't left angrily. I'd been well treated in that house, all things considered; I'd never been beaten, and I had repaid their generosity with hard work. We were pretty much even.

In a way, I learned what freedom was when I was with them. Because of my unusual birth, the family had never taken me to church. They told me I had to stay at the house to protect it from fire or robbers. When they went out, I played the piano as much as I wanted, I even played with the children's toys, which normally I wasn't allowed to touch; I looked at pictures in the storybook and I had whatever thoughts I liked. It was a kind of secret freedom, but freedom nonetheless.

The family had taught me a lot of other things too. I could wash and mend my clothes, thanks to the mother's instructions. I knew how to do everything that needed doing on a farm. I could even cook. I had the rudiments of baking, butchering, and carpentry. I therefore left them with more resources than I'd arrived with. Life had been as fair to me as it could have been.

What to do now? Well, for the moment, walk straight on. Something would turn up. Apart from the fact that I was famished, the idea of sleeping under the stars didn't bother me one little bit.

PART FOUR

I didn't have to go very far. The news that I had left my employer, and the reasons for my leaving, travelled swiftly, and were dissected, expanded, and twisted out of shape in less time than it's taken me to say it: the stupidity of the collective imagination is never idle. I was thrown out of the house because they caught me stealing, or I left because the father refused to let me marry his daughter—I heard it all over the next few months.

Anyway, about noon, a man in a buggy stopped and asked me if I was an honest man. I nodded, yes I was, and he asked me to climb aboard. I accepted his invitation, curious to know what he wanted. When we got to his farm, the last one before Cap-Lumière, he asked me whether I wanted to continue on by myself or stay and work for him. I was tempted to keep walking, but by this time I was too hungry to think straight. He offered me fifteen dollars a month with full room and board. I spent a few seconds tamping down the clothes in my rucksack. Then he raised the offer to eighteen dollars and added that I wouldn't have to live in the same house as the rest of the family unless I wanted to. I could stay in a fishing cabin that he had at the bottom of his property, near the river. For the first time in my life, I would have a place to myself. That's why I accepted his offer—that and the prospect of a hot meal.

I stayed with him for a little over three years. The man owned huge potato fields, and like everyone else he had a vegetable garden, an orchard, and a few farm animals. He was doing well, but he was greatly in need of a reliable farmhand. I started that same day, and since we were almost at the middle of the month, he gave me nine dollars on the spot, half of the monthly salary he'd promised me. Until that moment, I had never in my life had money of my own. His wife had a good heart too, and his children were polite, but what I liked best about their place was that no one there had known me as a boy; I felt as though I had always been a man for them. I'd had it with being a little hireling. Not only had leaving Sir erased my past, it had matured me in the eyes of others. Maybe that was why I've never liked staying in one place for too long. I like entering the lives of people as a complete unknown quantity, with no past, and not even a future. I hope to be able to go on like this for the rest of my days, wiping the slate clean every three or four years. You never get tired of life that way, and no one gets tired of you.

They let me eat at the table along with everyone else, and they served me first, like a guest. I never ate by myself unless they had company, in which case they asked me to eat before the others so as not to complicate matters. I didn't mind; I was happy to be treated as an employee rather than as a child to be pitied.

The best thing was the fishing cabin by the river. It was a simple-enough little set-up, with a bed, a stove, a table, two chairs, and an oil lamp. I painted the inside a colour I liked, and the lady of the house lent me some framed pictures to give the place a bit of life. I felt as though I was on constant vacation. I loved waking up alone in the morning and being alone after work; I could think, tell myself stories, and sleep peacefully. The workdays were sometimes brutal, but at night I was Lord and Master of my own domain, and I didn't need to scheme anymore to keep my position in the world. I froze at night in the wintertime, but I was never tempted to join the family like the hireling I used to be. I was happy to pay for my freedom with a bit of shivering.

In the winter, I worked in the logging camps in the bush and saved my wages, the equivalent of a year's salary in three months. The only luxuries I allowed myself were clothes that I bought once in a while—clothes that had never been worn by anyone else but me—my pipe tobacco, and all the lotions imaginable, a taste I had inherited from Papa: tooth lotion, hair lotion, aftershave lotion (even though I hardly ever shaved), and a powder that I put under my arms because the more cultivated ladies of my acquaintance seemed to appreciate it. I liked spending my nights arranging and rearranging my lotion bottles; it made me feel rich. I also liked a bit of perfume, and smelling clean on Sundays, my day off. In my former life, I'd had to work seven days a week. Here my Sundays and even my Saturday afternoons were my own.

With a dollar or two in my pocket, I would hang out from time to time at the general store that had once belonged to Sir, which I had never been allowed to enter when I was little, and where I couldn't have bought anything anyway since I never had any money. I spent long, delicious minutes looking at the little luxury items they had for sale: pocket knives, razors, tobacco pouches. I didn't often buy anything, but I could have if I'd wanted to. I actually preferred the bigger store in Baie-Sainte-Anne, the closest town to our farm, where I felt even freer because I didn't know a soul there. Getting to Baie-Sainte-Anne wasn't easy, but I managed to make the trek every spring and fall. The first big thing I bought was a tin filled with assorted candies, which I handed out to the children of the house because that's what I would have loved someone to have done for me when I was their age. Seeing their faces light up made me feel like a kid myself, but a kid who'd succeeded in life and had become a generous benefactor. I handed out gifts: I was rich.

One day I bought something for myself: the book of stories that the youngest daughter of my former employer used to read to me. It was exactly the same — bound in leather, with the same illustrations and everything. The saleslady congratulated me. "It's a good book, you'll see," she said. It was the kind of gift you buy for yourself when you're feeling down and out. With a book like that, you're never down, and you're never out.

My new employer taught me how to hunt and fish. Together, we would bring home plenty of hares, partridge, and trout. Sometimes we went all the way to the ocean to catch mackerel, which we put in the smoker or salted for the winter. We caught lobsters, which we brought back in cages for the dinners they held for their friends and his wife's family, because we lived in her part of the country, not his. He came from somewhere else, like me, and it's possible he felt a kind of kinship for me because of it: we were both living in exile, and we were both happy about it. Life here was much better than it had been back home.

Those were memorable feasts. We would roast a whole pig or a deer, and fill pots with fat to cook beans over the coals. And every meal was followed the next morning by huge, long, lazy breakfasts. We ate white bread with butter, and poured cream over fruit preserves that the wife made with berries she'd picked herself: blueberries, raspberries, strawberries, mulberries, blackcurrants. I often played the role of sous-chef because I loved watching the happy faces of people eating their fill.

There was one pleasure that had been unknown to me in my previous life: train tracks. The railway passed a few miles north of the farm.

The tracks were a gathering place for young people in the area who were "up to no good." The first time I heard that phrase was from my patron's wife, who was talking with her neighbour about the tracks and the dangers associated with them. She said the youngsters "did things" there, and certain young women had become pregnant; people went there to drink and smoke and swear and got into fights. I remember saying to myself: that's the place I absolutely have to go.

If you were brave enough to cross the mosquito-infested marsh on foot, you could head straight to the tracks and walk along them a ways until you ran into a few evening companions, boys and girls my own age who wanted to have a good time. I quickly made friends with them, all of us sharing what we brought. Someone produced a jug of homemade wine, someone else had cigarette tobacco and papers. The first time I went, I brought a bag of smoked herring and a few potatoes to roast, as well as a mickey of rum. The party got under way around a fire that we lit, even though it was a hot, humid summer's night, to keep the mosquitoes away. Some of us played music or sang. Those who could read called out the names of the cities painted on the sides of the railway cars as they went by. Everyone swore that they too would travel one day; I made the same promise to myself. We went home with bad breath from drinking cheap wine, our clothes damp with dew and stinking of tobacco smoke, and the vague certainty that we had tasted of forbidden pleasures.

The trains slowed down at the bottom of a steep hill, and it was there that tramps would jump into a boxcar to travel for nothing. I decided that, one day, that was how I would leave. I am my mother's son, I thought, I have inherited her need to keep a move on, to travel, to get myself lost. All I needed was a full rucksack and I could be gone for good. Not that I was unhappy where I was; I've been happy everywhere I've been, except for the prison and the insane asylum. But I knew that I could never remain in one place for long. All my life I've been like a ship happily drifting in search of ever more exotic shores.

That first night at the tracks, there were eight of us, four boys and four girls, and I was the only newcomer in the group. They talked non-stop, I recall, and their harangues, which I didn't always understand, were followed by long, happy silences. After a while, one of the boys and a girl stood up and wandered away, and the others wished them good luck and smiled knowingly. Then another couple drifted off, and the rest of us stayed around the fire, a bit ashamed of not being as bold as those who had left. I woke up in the morning with my hands and face swollen from mosquito bites, and a headache that felt as if I'd been run over by a train. But I was happy, truly happy, for the first time since my childhood.

We were a kind of secret society, a select club where young people could escape from their daily lives. We made friends on the spot, no one was turned away. In the villages where we lived and worked, we were young hooligans with no past and no future, like everyone else, but out at the tracks we were an elite corps. People talked about us, they feared us and whispered about us. But on the tracks, each of us was a someone, someone who lived above any law that applied to ordinary people; we obeyed no one's rules but our own, we were comrades in our little pleasures and our great expectations.

But what I liked most were the trains. When one passed that was a bit longer than the others, with the names of a dozen cities on its cars, the more experienced among us would explain where those mysterious places were, what kind of people lived in them, how far away they were. There were also freight trains, and the braver among us tried to find out what was in them and where they were going. These conversations fed my dreams of a future different from anything I had known before. The thoughts lifted me above the dull routines of my life, and each train always took me farther away from the little world I had known. One of these days I, a bold adventurer, would climb onto one of those trains and be gone, far, far away, and never again would I be alone with my thoughts and my dreams. I would dazzle others with tales of my adventures, which I would populate with eccentric but lovable characters. I wouldn't tell these stories myself, of course; surely others would tell them for me. I would become a legend. (Obviously, I did none of these things, but just dreaming about doing them freed me from the small world I'd been born into.)

I spent three summers at the tracks. We never went there in winter, only from May to October. You had to be a certain age to go there; partying along the tracks was not for adults, who would try to take advantage of our youthful innocence. A kind of purity of soul existed among us; we brought each other up, without interference from the outside.

Now that I think about it, it was a bit like school. The first summer, I was content to watch the others and imitate them. I learned to smoke and drink, for example. The second summer, I allowed myself my first taste of adult pleasures. The third summer, the older ones introduced me to new experiences. There was hardly ever a fourth summer; by then we were too old to be part of the inner group. Only losers tried to come for a fourth or fifth summer, and it didn't take them long to realize they were no longer welcome. You did your time at the tracks and then you swallowed your regrets and your remorse and moved on.

The parties themselves were far from innocent. They were the first time many of us had drunk ourselves into a stupor, or rolled our own cigarettes, or swore like troopers with perfect impunity. Often it was the first time that girls and boys were alone together, too. After discovering the joys of the flesh, we stopped hating our lives. Among themselves, the guys talked tough and dirty, in order to hide their doubts and fears; among themselves, the girls talked about love and the future, in order to hide their doubts and fears.

It was rare that the first time came during the first summer, but it was sure to come during the second. My first summer, I wasn't completely trusted, I wasn't well-enough known; for all they knew, I'd only be there once and then I'd bugger off, so they waited to see if I would come back a second time. They had to give me a name, a story, a reputation. A guy had to show he was tough without being mean, that he had a sense of humour and behaved himself, that he would share everything he had and also keep to himself from time to time, and skip his turn. We never fought among ourselves, we ganged up only on those who came to cause trouble. That's the usual thing for all young men. I never had to fight once. Papa taught me that, in a fight, the stronger of the two is always the one who defends himself. I've had to defend myself a few times in my life, but I've never attacked anyone.

The third summer was filled with the sadness of the last summer of youth: there were frequent ruptures between lovers, partners changed, the faces of those we loved and those we didn't much like disappeared; we stopped playing certain games, the old codes to which we had clung with such ferocity now began to get on our nerves, suddenly appearing childish to us. It was the same for me as for the others. The roads around the tracks transported us from youthful bliss to the helpless state of watching our youth slip away.

The second summer was the sweetest.

They called her Freckles, because she had red hair and her body was liberally sprinkled with red spots. She wasn't exactly pretty. The best you could say about her was that she was endowed with that forthright confidence that often compensates those who aren't thought to be beautiful. That's what appealed to me when I first laid eyes on her. Tall and strong, she protected the younger girls from the more aggressive guys who came around the tracks, and I found that bigness of spirit attractive. She dreamed of having a boyfriend, just one, someone she would call her lover, but she was prepared to take her time finding the right one. She knew she had to wait her turn, because prettier girls were always the first to be chosen.

Not a single guy looked at her or even called her by her real name. Paying attention to her was simply not done. The other girls often made fun of her because of her physical awkwardness and her braying laugh. And everyone gave her a hard time because of her smell, which I had to admit was strong. My first thought was that she wasn't likely to turn me away. I was in the same boat as her: the pretty girls would have nothing to do with a guy who didn't talk, but like Freckles, I knew that my turn would come. The first time our eyes met, we knew we were co-conspirators.

One moonless night when we were sitting around the campfire, after our ritual singing and passing around of the bottle of dandelion wine, we heard the long, mournful whistle of a passing train. The group jumped up and ran off to watch it climb the long hill beside us. I stayed where I was, poking at the fire in a preoccupied fashion. She stayed behind too, her head lowered. The others didn't come back; you'd swear they knew that our time had come.

She spoke first in the darkness, her back to the fire. She told me that two years before, four or five guys from her village, men who were too big or too old to come to the tracks, had held her down and took turns fucking her as if she were some kind of whore. She wanted me to know what had happened, she said, and she began to cry. "That's why the guys here don't like me, because I'm spoiled goods... The girls don't like me because I wasn't able to get away..." I took her in my arms to let her know that I didn't think she was spoiled goods, and she pressed herself against me to dry her tears. Our mouths met, and soon we were stretched out on the ground, me on top of her, clinging to each other so tightly we almost did it that night.

It was almost midnight when I walked her home, our arms around each other's waist. It was raining a bit, but we hardly noticed. We had each other, we each existed for another in our flesh, as if we were the first creatures to be alive on this planet, and we stopped every five minutes to exchange the kisses we were certain we had just invented.

The next Saturday, I didn't go to the tracks. I waited for her at my place. I had drawn a map for her showing how to find it. She didn't turn up. I told myself my desire for her was too beautiful to be true.

Her cries woke me up in the middle of the night. She had been following the river and become lost on the tidal flats, and was calling to me for help. I lit a fire beside the cabin so she could see where it was, and when she finally came towards me, I ran out to meet her. The sight of her helpless, relieved face evoked a mixture of pity and desire in me, a complicated blend. I invited her into my cabin, and we finally became man and woman. She liked giving pleasure, and so did I. Men and women not naturally endowed with looks are more generous with their bodies and their actions than those who are conscious of their own beauty. She left early the next morning. She didn't want to stay, she didn't even eat anything, saying she had to get home before her family noticed she was missing. She was afraid of being called a slut, she said. I walked her out to the main road, and as she left, she said she would come back. I smiled to let her know that she would be very welcome.

She never had been raped by the guys at the tracks; that was one of the stories people in the area told to keep their virtuous daughters from going there. She told it to boys she met in order to make them feel sorry for her, so that, like me, they would be kinder to her, try to erase that bad memory from her life. I didn't blame her, of course; I even admired her tactical genius.

She came back fairly often, enough for us to get pretty good at making love. Someone else might have found her odour off-putting, but not me. It was hard to describe; it reminded me of some kind of animal fat burning on a stove. She told me I smelled of the farm and of silt from the river, and that together we smelled like a couple of fish out of water.

I discovered the source of her odour when she asked me to walk her all the way home because she was afraid of going by herself. It was the end of summer, and there were bears wandering about in the woods.

She lived in a ramshackle house that was badly in need of repair, with mud-covered children running about the yard and their mother, a cigarette jutting out from the corner of her mouth, sitting on a stump plucking wild ducks. Her father was butchering something in the living room. Through the window, I could see sides of pork and moose hanging from the ceiling. He was boiling pig's blood on the stove to make blood pudding, and asked us if we were hungry. Freckles said we were. Her father poured some molasses into the steaming pot, and after stirring it for a while, he transferred the mess into a large bowl of gruel. We ate from unwashed plates, but the bread was good. Before joining us at the table, he offered me a glass of homemade whisky. After the meal, he went back to his butchery in the living room, and I watched him make blood pudding with help from his wife, who didn't speak any more than I did. That was the day I realized why my lover smelled so strongly. The whole family smelled as she did, of spices mixed with pork blood. I'd have smelled like her if I spent much time at her place.

By introducing me to her family, she let me know that she was not ashamed of me, which made me feel good. And by offering me a glass of whisky, her father treated me like a grown-up. For the first time since the auction separated me from my first family, I felt as if I existed in the eyes of someone other than myself; I was no longer alone in my head. With a full stomach, still a little woozy from the whisky, I made every promise to life and the world that a man in love is capable of making.

We were together until early winter. I would climb into my little rowboat on Sunday mornings and let the outgoing tide carry me to the place where she lived. I'd come back home on the incoming tide. I liked her family. They always made me feel welcome, and Freckles liked being seen with me. She was happy to finally have someone who was interested in more than just screwing her by the side of the tracks, someone who came to see her for no other reason than to be with her.

Winter set in, and in the spring she didn't go back to the tracks. One Sunday, I borrowed my employer's horse and buggy and went to see her. There was no one at her house. A neighbour told me that the family had gone into town for the day.

I never saw her again. Her family had got her a job as a housemaid in town, so she could send them money. Two of her friends took her place in my cabin. They were tough-headed women who liked a roll in the hay and talking like longshoremen, like many young women born into poverty who think their asses are their best features. I readily admit that I liked listening to them, especially the prettier of the two, whose frank way of speaking I found strangely erotic. The other one was the quiet type: she liked to watch.

By my third summer at the tracks, I had become a kind of mentor to the newcomers as well as to those who knew me. I was almost twenty, verging on an old man. I performed little services for people. I calmed them down when a fight erupted; I treated their cuts and bruises; I lit the fire; I had food when they were hungry; and I had the best bootleg rum because, compared with everyone else, I was rich. Everything was going well. I had earned my stripes.

That year, after the potatoes were harvested and bagged, and after the usual festival that followed it, my employer asked me if I would stay another year. I shook my head no. He asked me all kinds of questions to find out why. I asked one of the children who was drawing at the table to lend me a sheet of paper and a crayon, and I drew a train. When the wife saw my drawing, she turned to her husband and said: "Let him go. He likes it here, it seems, but you can't stop a young man from wanting to see the world. We're his only family, but he's much too young to let himself be buried alive here. His time has come. There's no more risk of him being sent to the orphanage—he can go where he pleases. The police won't pick him up for being a vagrant; he has money, and he could use it to settle down, or at least that's what he could tell them he intends to do. And if he's arrested, we'll testify on his behalf. Let him go. We'll find someone else." This woman, who in the three years I'd been living there hadn't spoken more than three words to me, understood me better than I understood myself. It felt good to be understood without having to explain myself.

The next morning, dressed in a new suit of clothes that no one had ever worn before, carrying a suitcase that held nothing but what belonged to me, my pockets full of money I'd earned myself, I set out on my journey of adventure, this time for real. I'm still on it.

The morning I left, my boss drove me to the train station. It was hard, separating myself from the family, especially from the children, who cried their eyes out. I cried too, inside. What moved me most was the neatly tied package the wife handed me at the door, which turned out to contain enough food to last me two days.

Alone at the station, I spent two hours studying the map of the province that hung from the wall, and with the help of a travelling salesman who was only too happy to read it to me, I found the place where I'd been born and bought a ticket for a train going in the opposite direction. I must have had an instinct for protecting myself, although from what I don't know. What I do know is that all my life I've rarely returned to a place where I've been happy, where people have been good to me. I've never wanted anyone who knew me to remember who I was. I'd rather fade from their memories and let them go on living in mine. I want to be the only flesh-and-blood being in my world of kindly shadows.

And I've stuck to that. My whole life, all I've ever done is pass through.

PART FIVE

This morning, when the bailiff came by to make an inventory of the family's worldly goods, the husband took off, and I was afraid his wife would die of shame. She shouted at the children to get out of the house, no doubt to spare them having to watch the bailiff doing his job. The children were obviously rattled, so I took them down to the stream to show them how to fish for trout before the season opens in a few days. But they understand what's going on; they don't need anyone to tell them. I hope for their sakes it'll be over soon.

I went for a walk afterwards, because that's the way I am, and my steps took me to Cap-Pelé. The few people I met on the road looked away when they saw me, further evidence that the auction isn't far off. I felt like a condemned man on his way to the scaffold, or like I was carrying some kind of infectious disease. I noticed someone had pinned a notice up on the church door. I sat on a bench in the little garden opposite, in the hopes that some kind soul would come and read it to me.

A young, well-dressed man came out of the church with a preoccupied air. I thought he must be the new priest; the old one's just retired. I placed myself in his path and showed him the notice. He shook his head and murmured something that sounded like, "I couldn't agree with you more, sir! A barbaric custom... Soon, when I'm in charge here, there'll be no more of these human auctions..." I couldn't hold him back, he was in such a hurry. I sat back down on the bench and waited for someone else to come by.

Suddenly, the doctor's housekeeper appeared, hurrying towards her car, which was parked in front of the church. I stood up as she approached, and I could see right away that she regretted the coincidence that I was finding so delightful. She tried to go around me, but without a moment's hesitation I took her by the arm and led her gently to the notice. It was obvious she had already read it, and that she would have given anything to be somewhere else. I looked at her insistently: "Read it, madame, please," I said with my eyes. "Out loud, if it isn't too much trouble."

She read it, and her emotional state moved me. When I thanked her by nodding my head, she looked into my eyes for a long time, hers filling with tears, and I reassured her by taking her hand. She regained her calm and, patting me on the arm, left with a dignified step.

The auction will be held this Saturday, at three o'clock. The day after tomorrow. It will be outdoors, behind the church, after the market closes. There'll be four of us: a woman, two older men, and me. At five o'clock there will also be a children's auction, which is unusual because normally they don't hold two sessions on the same day. So there's sure to be a large crowd, the housekeeper said, and the weather's supposed to be fine.

I know the woman who's being auctioned. She lives on the farm next to ours; the family she's with has been talking for a long time about getting rid of her because she's cranky. She tries to boss everyone around, she yells at the children, she refuses to eat the same things as everyone else at the table, and sometimes she doesn't leave her room for days, not even to go to the toilet. The family has had enough. That's what everyone says, which means it's almost certainly not true.

I also know one of the men fairly well. Until a short while ago he was a prosperous farmer and was treated with a great deal of respect when he visited Cap-Pelé. I don't know what happened to make his children abandon him. I'd like to find out; surely he'll tell us all about it, complete with certain facts added and others left out. The other old man is from a different parish. I don't know anything about him, but he worries me. Chances are he's a proper old gent who's holding up well, has just landed here by chance, is more vigorous than me, and has the added advantage of speaking, so can tell stories to children about the good old days that'll make them grow up wise before their time. If that's the case, he'll be going home with the best family, that's for sure.

Anxiety gnaws at me like a rat. Is anyone going to take me? Or will they prefer the mysterious stranger? I might as well admit it: I'm secretly hoping the housekeeper will come back and bid on me, and it's this hope that is causing me such anguish, because I know how unlikely it is. I can't imagine such a distinguished lady taking an old duffer like me home, dressed in her deceased brother-in-law's suit, no less. She'd be the laughingstock of the whole town. She'd bring me back to the next auction and I'd be laughed at even more. Of course she'll go for the other guy, the one I don't know, if only for appearances' sake. Or maybe the cranky old woman, out of charity. I'll probably be the last one taken, or I may not be taken at all, which will mean it's the old folks' home for me. Or else the highway.

There's one thing that pleases me about the notice, though: for once in my life I'm being called by my real name, the one my mother gave me at my birth.

I'm not proud of it, but I'm the only member of my family who's been sold at auction. The first time, there was nothing I could do about it; the second time, I was there of my own free will. This time, I'll be somewhere in between.

My mother would rather have killed herself than be auctioned off. She was from a family that had been independent since Noah was in diapers. She wasn't an orphan, as some have suggested. On the contrary, she knew her real parents. When she was born, her clan lived on the Bay of Fundy, not far from Rockport, on fish they drew from the sea and the tidal rivers. Her people farmed the land as well, but fitfully—potatoes, beets. They also picked wild berries, which grew like weeds throughout the region. After that, her clan travelled a lot—into the interior, up into the hills, down into the wetlands, and all along the coast. She had relatives in the cities too, in the ports, the harbours, and even in other countries. They never stayed in one place for long; I wouldn't stay in one place for more than four or five hundred years either, if I was them. My family hunted and trapped wherever the land permitted it. My mother knew everything the members of her clan knew, and passed her knowledge down to me. I've inherited centuries of silent wisdom from her.

The history of her clan is like a scar that runs across the side of a mountain, sometimes almost dropping out of sight, other times standing out like a sore thumb. Whether you notice it or not doesn't matter, but don't make fun of it, or insult it — or, worse, pretend it doesn't exist. It'll spew venom and blood, and bad memories will fly out of it like deformed demons, looking to sow evil.

One day, some government agents arrived in the marsh where the clan had been living for two generations. They built a fort that had a dispensary and a few offices, then they left. Missionaries took their place. They wanted the children to go to school, they said, but they didn't stay long either. They built a church, but it was struck by lightning and burned to the ground. Since there were no more agents or missionaries around, the family dismantled the fort and burned the wood in their fireplaces during the winter. After that, there was endless bickering among them, quarrels fed by greed, jealousy, and alcohol. The clan began to break up, led by those who had horses and could find work in the North. These horse-people were known to be hard workers; they slept under their mounts, wrapped in multicoloured blankets, and asked only to be given food and paid. They were hard drinkers too, both the men and the women. By the time my mother was born, there were only two or three families left in the marsh. Hers still lived there despite the fact that the bush was quickly reclaiming the fields around them. All that remained of the clan were their memories and their name. They were called the

People of the Marsh, or the People of the Sea, or sometimes the People of the River, through their connection with our cousins from the North. No one was sure of their real name, not even them. When my mother was little, the area became less and less inhabitable because of winter storms that ravaged the last of the arable lands. In the spring, it was easier to find semi-precious stones on the land than it was to grow turnips and potatoes.

My mother's father was a fisherman and a smuggler—mostly a smuggler. He had a few run-ins with the law, but he never went to prison. He was the best moose-caller in the area; his imitation of a female moose in heat would bring the males running out of the woods like lumberjacks on payday. Thanks to him, there was never a shortage of meat in the marsh. One day he disappeared without a trace. Seems he couldn't stand his wife anymore. She could kill with her voice too, because she knew how to cast spells on people and tell the kind of truths that made their souls tremble for the rest of their lives; the memory of her sharp tongue sometimes made her victims want to kill themselves. She never had a good word to say about anyone, and everyone hated her, even though as a young girl she'd been one of the most beloved of the clan women. No one knew where her bitterness came from, and her children were afraid of growing up to be like her. She died of a fever one winter night, abandoned by everyone. She wasn't even buried; they just took her body and threw it into the marsh somewhere to sink out of sight. My mother and her brothers and sisters were taken away by government agents, since there was no one else to look after them. They weren't sorry to go; they'd had enough of being the children of a man and a woman who could maim and kill with their voices.

My mother stayed on in the Grande-Digue orphanage; the others were dealt out to a number of different families. None of them ever went up for auction, because no one would want one of the Marsh People—they'd just run away. My mother was separated from her brothers and sisters for a long time. When she met up with them again, later in life, they didn't seem related to her. Their collective memory had faded and they no longer had anything in common.

My mother hated the orphanage, and she handed her defiance of all walled-in institutions down to me. She missed her family, was even nostalgic for the foul smells she grew up with, the simple games she played with the neighbour kids, the freedom of having what was needed for their unique existence: a roof over their heads, enough to eat and drink. And she missed the marsh, where she'd sought refuge whenever she was troubled, and the pink light that the sun breathed over the empurpled land. I love that light too; it's the same light we have here. I'd have a hard time giving it up. It may be why I like being a stranger in my own country; I wouldn't feel comfortable any other way.

But there were things she liked about the orphanage, even if she didn't like to admit it; she never made concessions to anyone. For example, the new name she took for herself: Salomé. The name hadn't come easily, however. At her arrival, she was told she was going to be baptized, and she kicked up the kind of holy terror that only she was capable of. To calm her down, the sister in charge of the kitchen, who was also from the marshes but had the good sense not to tell anyone, took her out into the orphanage garden. There was a small cemetery next to it, between the orphanage and the river, and when the young girl noticed that there were words carved into the head-stones — names, they must have been — the sister set about reading them to her, as a kind of game. The girl said she liked the name Salomé. And so the sister told her she could take it, if she wanted it. "You're old enough to choose your own name," she said. "Salomé can be your baptismal name." That promise was enough to make her listen to reason: she took the name the way a child grabs an abandoned toy. She went back inside with the sister and was baptized on the spot. The other sisters accepted her choice without comment; the descendants of a conquered people are usually fond of exotic-sounding words, and avenge themselves for their ancestors' defeat by uncon-sciously appropriating the illustrious past of their conquerors. They give themselves the names of dethroned emperors, dead queens, and illustrious savants. The girl who had the bed on Salomé's left in the dormitory was named Cleopatra, and the one on the right was Marie-Antoinette. The gardener and factotum of the orphanage was named Euclid.

The newly christened Salomé tried to run away three times in her first year, probably out of instinct. She never got very far. But she refused to learn to read or write or do sums, no matter what the nuns did. She enjoyed sewing and working in the kitchen, though. After a while, she got used to orphanage life and understood that she would get out sooner if she behaved herself. One day, she overheard someone saying about her that she had a good heart and her head screwed on right, and that she would do well in life. That was when she realized that the orphanage door would open only if she took every opportunity to demonstrate her worth. She decided to seize the first chance that came along. Until then, she'd be patient.

When she grew too old to stay in the orphanage, she was placed with a family in Pré-d'en-Haut, where there were others of her age. It was a good family, and even though she kept her distance from them, she was happy enough there. She only needed to bide her time for a while and soon she would be free for good. She wasn't very clear about where she would go; all she knew for certain was that she would travel as far away as she could get and never come back.

A taste for men developed early in her, and made her put her plans on hold. As soon as she entered puberty, she began to seek out the pleasures of male company, and everyone in the parish talked about the beautiful Salomé. She herself was amazed at the change that came over her: the thin little girl with the hungry eyes had become a voluptuous woman, with shining hair and a soft, dark gaze that could hypnotize even men whose own tastes were not for women.

One day, she told me, she thought it might be easier to get away if she had someone to go with her. A man, for example, who wanted to travel across land and sea, far from where she was, far from everything she had known. With such a man, she would have children who would never end up in an orphanage, like her.

Her family advised her to have a care for her virtue, but she laughed that off. As a young girl she had often seen her parents going at it night and day, and she saw no reason why she should act any differently. Her detractors began to murmur that she had the devil in her, and that men would be wise to steer clear of her. She let comments like that roll off her back, and kept her head up. "Let them gossip all they want," she would say. "I may not have much, but one thing I do have is class." She didn't quite know what she meant by that—it must have been something she'd heard somewhere—but the statement had more truth to it than she knew.

Her eyes would widen when she saw any boy who pleased her, but she only had eyes for one, and she dreamed of him at night when she was alone in her bed. She was at that tender age when we fall in love at the drop of a hat, when torments of the heart come and go like the dew.

I know all this because I already existed within her. I could hear her most intimate thoughts, and experience all the feelings that flowed through her body. I was there, entirely formed in spirit, as silent then as I am today.

By the time I appeared in Salomé's body, I was endowed with memory and speech. I was pre-existent, with three thousand years of memories stored up in me. I was in my mother long before she became a woman, I knew her parents and all her kin long before she did. I spoke to her when she was still a child, and at first she would listen without saying a word. She could hear my voice, and she would speak to me when she played with her doll or ignore me when she was tired.

Because she knew I was inside her, she never felt alone. When her family broke up, she found comfort in my company. I was the source of the calmness in her that passed for toughness, a reproach that never bothered her because she knew she possessed a truth that very few others are aware of.

Of course, I couldn't enter this world without the connivance of a man. As soon as Salomé became a woman, she had only to look at a boy or a man to know if the other half of me was in him. She also knew that it was written somewhere that I was the last of her clan, and so she had no choice but to get me out into the world. She began actively seeking me the moment she felt her first flush of desire, when she was twelve years old, and she already had a good idea of what kind of person I would turn out to be. But her longing for me was a secret; she never mentioned me to a soul.

Her first love was a boy totally different from her. It was customary for People of the Marsh and People of the River to mix with others from away, so it wasn't unusual for her to set her sights on this fair-haired, grey-eyed prince.

Naturally, she was first attracted to him by the things he had that she didn't. Things count for a lot more than personality when you don't know much about your body. He wore ties because his mother was determined that he dress like a gentleman in order to look more serious, which she thought would help him get on with people of means. The tie was green, which brought out his freckles, an unknown trait among the People of the Marsh. When winter arrived, she swooned over the brand new ice skates that his parents had bought for him from a catalogue. The young man was their only child. He was intelligent and would go to college, they said, and so he'd eventually have even more things that Salomé didn't have.

All the time she was in love with him, she never looked at another man. He was unaware that she was faithful to him; she herself didn't even realize it. She'd only spoken to him once, at the church bazaar in Memrancook, where she said hello to him in his own language, maybe a touch loud because she'd been rehearsing it for days. The youngsters around them broke out laughing. "Well, I'd say the Gypsy has taken a shine to you!" (They called her the Gypsy because of her dark complexion, but it didn't bother her. She even liked it, with its hint of worldliness and travel.) Everyone in the village found the anecdote funny, and went around repeating it with glee, although not maliciously. Salomé was the first to admit that her skin was dark, that she was too poor and uneducated to even have the right to look at the Young Prince (which is what she always called him in her heart of hearts, but never in front of others). But she was convinced that such obstacles were just extra reasons for loving him. That mad ache caused by her first tumble only strengthened her resolve to stick with a man who was different from her.

The Young Prince was a good fellow, and was flattered that such a beautiful young woman would be interested in him. One day when he was skating on the frozen river, he waved at her and called out her name, which she didn't hear because the wind was blowing too hard, but she was sure she had read it on his lips, even though she couldn't read.

"Salomé..."

From that moment on, she decided to keep that name even after she returned to the People of the Marsh. Her name, uttered by the mouth of her beloved, had enriched her life. She no longer confused things and people in her mind. She didn't see the young man's green tie and skates, only the skater's face as the cold sketched her name in the air as it flew from his wind-whitened lips.

I probably shouldn't mention this, but immediately after the Young Prince called her name, his foot caught in a crack in the ice. He tried to recover his lost balance, did that little dance called the angel's jig, and ended up sitting on his backside on the ice. For the rest of her life, Salomé would remember how that one unfortunate detail tarnished her first tender memory.

But this dazzling, hopeless love was too painful to last for very long. What was more, I was not in him, and Salomé knew it. She refused to believe it in her heart, but her body knew; I knew it too. In any case, the Young Prince left. His family decided to send him to the seminary to become a priest. It was assumed in the parish that that would be only a first step, that he would be a bishop one day, or else would marry a rich, devoted young woman and live in a great mansion with a dozen servants like Salomé. One night towards the end of August, a sumptuous feast was held to mark his departure, to which all the notables in the region were invited.

It was then that Salomé made her first and only social mistake: she declared out loud that she was going to the soirée. In her innocence, she thought that since she was in love with the Young Prince and he was evidently enamoured of her, there would be no harm in her going. The young women with her that day in the garden behind the church laughed at her audacity, and when she asked them why they were making fun of her, they said straight off that she didn't belong in that world, she didn't have enough class. The explanation intrigued more than wounded her.

What Salomé didn't know was that the young man's father belonged to a family that had once owned vast domains and had lost them when the popular will wrested power from the wealthy elite that had controlled New Brunswick since the colonial period. At the family's peak, the patriarch had been elected to the legislative assembly, but after a brilliant political debut he was defeated and had to content himself with the post of customs officer, a sinecure he could hardly see as anything but a consolation prize. The mother was a former local beauty, also from a distinguished family whose hour of glory had come and gone. Her misfortune had landed her the job of postmistress, another compensation for her family's loss of prestige. The two jobs guaranteed them a comfortable income, rare in those parts, but the couple preferred to dwell on memories of the faded grandeur of their families, whose power had been swept away by the ill winds of fairness and equality. And that's exactly what is meant by class: the memory of a noble failure that you wear like armour to distinguish yourself from your less deserving new masters. It's the refuge of all your shipwrecked ambitions, individual or collective, the excuse you use to explain your exclusion from all those you judge to be unworthy of their share of the bitter delights of defeat, glorious or inglorious. This notion of class therefore creates only harmless inequalities, perpetuated by the illusion of a greatness brought low by means of democratic virtues. But these truths were inaccessible to Salomé, blinded as she was by the worldly glamour and the promise of happiness she saw in the eyes of a fifteen-year-old boy.

In the end, Salomé changed her mind about turning up uninvited at the ball. She didn't want to spoil her Young Prince's debut into society. But she couldn't resist the temptation to hide in the nearby bushes, and for the entire evening tears she believed to be the last in her body poured out of her. It was over, love had had its day and then perished. In the aftermath, she managed to find some consolation in the vague notion that everything great and beautiful and noble in life has its origins in a game of lost love. Her exclusion was proof to her that she existed, and that existence always demanded a price. But she refused to wear widow's weeds, knowing instinctively that such vain ornamentation serves only to satisfy false heroes, imagined victims, and true failures—in other words, all those who have nothing but aborted histories with which to puff themselves up. No one would ever see that she'd been wounded in love.

Her pain was great, however, and it opened a hole in her heart so huge that it could be filled by anyone who came along. She took up with a young lout from the area whom she had turned away a dozen times already, a tall idiot with a large head of hair whose physical strength masked his profound stupidity. She stayed with him long enough to know what deep kisses tasted like, and how it felt to have her body caressed by another's hands. When he tried to force himself upon her one night, she kept him at bay by resorting to a string of insults she'd learned from her mother that she thought she'd forgotten. Her attacker was so stunned by her vehemence that he shook every time he remembered her words, and for a long time afterwards was unable to get an erection.

Disappointed, she gave up all dealings with men for life, and I didn't hear her even mention them for the longest time. Her body was resting from its first amorous exertions, its first disappointments. She decided to return to her family, the People of the Marsh, and secretly packed her bag. We would be hitting the road, which was fine by me.

Her plans were in place by the time the harvest started and the first workers appeared from the fishing villages along the coast and the settlements in the interior, in search of work and amusement. The region was full of young men who, sitting around their campfires in the evenings, told strange and enticing stories that everyone already knew by heart but everyone wanted to hear again. Among them were former residents of the marshes who lived apart from the other workers, preferring to sleep under their horses. Salomé loved to search them out and talk to them about this and that, to show them how much she had changed.

Among those who came from farther away was one a little older and more serious than the others. He was twenty-three, married, with a child. He owned a house in the hills, somewhere near Néguac, with a garden and a chicken coop. He had to leave his young family twice each year, to work in the fields in the summer and to cut wood in the bush during the winter months. As soon as he earned enough to keep his family for a year, he went home to play with his child, he said, and to tend his garden. He never spoke just to hear the sound of his own voice, and he played the violin and the harmonica like a pro.

Often, around the bonfire they lit each night, the men told stories about what they would do with all the money they were going to make that year. Nearly all of them talked about what they intended to buy, but this young man never said a word. Except once: "One day," he said, "when I have enough money, I'll bring my daughter into town and have her picture taken. I'll put the picture in my wallet and it'll be with me wherever I go, and when I miss her, I'll just take out her photo and look at it and talk to her." The others looked away as if he had said something embarrassing, but Salomé listened carefully and began feeling a new emotion. She thought she would have loved to have had a father like him, who would think of her like that. She wanted to know a man like that. Sitting there in the darkness, she felt herself getting warm, and began to feel soft and humid inside, and taken by shivers down her spine, just above her buttocks. She didn't know what it was until later: it was the first time she'd felt desire for a man.

She began to edge towards him, imperceptibly, instinctively, irresistibly, a woman as aware of what she was doing as one who'd been doing it all her life. She wanted him, she had decided. Reserved as he was, she had a hard time winning him over, and since she knew none of a woman's artful ways, she tried coming right out and telling him what she wanted: "I'd like us to sleep together." He resisted for a long time, a very long time, afraid he would no longer desire his own wife if he went with this young woman, because he'd heard that infidelity causes impotence in a man and indifference in a woman. Salomé swept his arguments aside with a gesture:

"All you have to do is think of her when you're inside me. As if I'm taking her place. I'll think about us enough for both of us. And I promise I won't try to keep you afterwards." In the end he gave in, telling himself that being the first man in Salomé's life would be good for her in the long run, and since he was such a generous guy.

They met one cool night in an abandoned barn where she'd set up a makeshift bed. The mosquitoes weren't too bad and blackfly season was over. At first she was surprised and disappointed that she didn't feel more, but she was a devoted student and he was a conscientious teacher, and after a few nights the memory of their first encounter vanished in the fervour of their subsequent meetings. Before knowing him, Salomé had viewed lovemaking as a simple, ugly, but necessary formality, no doubt influenced by her mother, who delighted in dirtying every glimmer of human happiness with her bitter tongue. Now she saw their fondling in a new and beauteous light, every gesture a kind of offering and prayer, each look they exchanged ennobling them. They soon became dedicated lovers. Each night was better than the one before. She loved falling asleep in his strong arms, revelling in the aroma of spent love, convinced she would rather the world came to an end than that she would have to live in it without him.

She didn't know it then, but those were her halcyon days. The unhappiness she experienced later in life would never dull the memory of them. Not even in death would she forget their time together.

I know about this episode because, when she was an adult and a mother, she liked to climb into bed with my aunt and the two would talk about men and love. My half-sister slept in the next bed, and I would close my eyes the better to hear what they were saying.

Salomé always hated to hear a man described as being good in bed. Not just because she thought the expression vulgar, but because, as she would say, "No one is a good lover by himself. You can only be good in bed if there are two of you." And my aunt would nod gravely, as if she agreed completely. I don't know how much she understood, and I contented myself with filing Salomé's words away until I was able to understand them at some future juncture.

"But real pleasure," my aunt would ask her, "what exactly is it?" It was a difficult question, and Salomé could only answer by saying, "It depends on the woman—it's not the same for all of us. For me, it's like having bees buzzing all over my body, going from one part of me to the next, and feeling full of honey afterwards, like my blood is so thick I'll never be able to walk straight again. I want to limp with love for the rest of my life, happy to the bone to stay in that altered state forever, and every time I have to go back to being what I was before, I can hardly stand it." My aunt would then say: "Yes, yes! I can see that! That's just the way it is! Just listening to you, I can feel my blood turning into honey. When you talk like that, Salomé, it's like it's happening to me..." Then the two women would be quiet for a long time, each absorbed in her own memories of a few beautiful moments that had meant so much to them.

Once, my aunt took the conversation further. "Do you sometimes think," she asked, "that doing it is wrong? That maybe it's kind of dirty?"

"No," Salomé assured her, "it's never dirty. It's only ugly if you don't want to do it, if the man forces himself on you. Otherwise it's beautiful, so beautiful and pleasurable it can never be dirty."

My aunt seemed satisfied. She went to sleep, and Salomé, still aroused, got dressed and went out into the night. This happened more than once.

I learned about other things by listening when Salomé talked to herself. What surprised her most about the business was that she had learned to like herself. Before falling in love, she had never liked her own body; she thought it was badly put together. And she liked men's bodies even less. But being the focus of a lover's rapt attentions had awakened her, and she was no longer the same person, not the same person at all.

And so she went from discovery to discovery, each one more pleasurable than the last. There was happiness to experience in life after all, there was such a thing as an earthly paradise, God existed, and He must be good to have invented so many pleasures that she hadn't known about. She had never felt so loving, so full, so generous. The feeling of being loved made her a moral person, and from then on she would have her eyes wide open, blessed by rain as well as by sun, eager to learn the names of all the flowers and birds. The ugliness of the world disappeared, and she exuded only beauty and goodness.

She would recount these revelations to her exhausted lover in the middle of the night. He never said anything. He'd promised himself he'd stay only long enough to initiate Salomé into the mysteries of married life, and here he was, almost unable to remember the features of the woman he'd left behind, and the thought troubled him. One morning he even had to think long and hard to remember his wife's name. Deeply disturbed, he was glad the harvest was going smoothly, so that he would soon be able to go home.

It didn't take long for Salomé to see that he was on the point of leaving her, and she felt a sting of resentment towards him she would regret until her dying day. She was the one who had dragged him into this, after all, and also the one who had gone back on her word. Her mother began to visit her in her dreams, even during the day, still as foul-mouthed as ever, maligning each and every amorous attachment: "Do his feet not stink, this lover of yours? What's his breath like in the morning? I suppose he shits like everyone else? And it smells as bad as yours does, does it not? You poor idiot, still filling your head with ideas." At such times Salomé found herself cursing her lover, accusing him of all sorts of vileness. He never replied in anger; he even took her insults with a kind of relief, because they made it easier for him to look forward to getting back to his wife, whom he'd all but forgotten in Salomé's whimpering gratitude.

For weeks on end, she'd found herself smiling from morning till night, believing herself the luckiest woman alive. Now she was the unhappiest of creatures. In her more lucid moments she asked herself how she could have sunk from such a peak of joy to such depths of misery.

When he finally did leave, she felt more relief than pain. At least the constant torture was over. He passed her house one morning and waved goodbye, but she held herself back from calling out his name. If she thought the pain would leave her, though, she was wrong. On the contrary, it was only beginning; she soon understood the tales she had heard about lovers who kill themselves for love. Her confusion was so deep that she felt she was leading a double life: on the outside she was a dutiful, conscientious young woman who did her work well, while inside she was a child-woman cruelly deprived of her lover's gentle touch and comforting words.

What hurt her most were all the thoughts spinning around in her head. "If he had simply abandoned me, at least he'd be suffering from a bad conscience, and I'd be able to take some pleasure from that," she told herself. "And if he'd rejected me, I could hate him and punish him by taking up with another man who was worse than him." But he hadn't abandoned or rejected her, he'd simply gone home because he felt obliged to, and his absence had thrown her back on herself: he had taken her heart with him, leaving her vulnerable, with a full heart and an empty nest, ceaselessly tormented by her mother's laughter and viciousness ringing again in her ears.

All her confusion, however, disappeared as quickly as it had come. One fall morning, when she was doing the washing outside, she felt an urgent need and had to go behind the stable to relieve it. It took her longer than usual, and suddenly she felt something happening in her innards, something soft, like an egg yolk breaking inside her without making a sound. What came out was an oddly shaped thing that looked like a tadpole, or some other kind of amphibian. She looked at it for a few minutes, then with the tenderest of care she wrapped it in a rhubarb leaf and set it aside so she could examine it more closely later on. But the next day she couldn't bring herself to look at it again, and found herself crying for no apparent reason. She wrapped the thing, whatever it was, in a white cloth and buried it near her favourite red oak, in the bush beside the house.

That night, an older friend of hers remarked that she was looking paler than usual. Salomé told her she'd been bleeding for a while. Without asking any further questions, the woman told her of an infusion of raspberry leaves that was known to restore the intimate health of a woman. For weeks Salomé drank the tea as if in a trance, prey to a vagueness of soul that she'd never known before. The woman told her she'd had a miscarriage, but Salomé mentioned it to no one. In the days that followed, she often thought of the little being that had lived so briefly inside her body. She had delivered me for the first time.

It took her a while to realize that her mother was no longer torturing her day and night with her vicious words attacking all men and the women who loved them. From then on, a certain amount of peace of mind settled over her. Her new-found taste for men left her, her suffering ended, and she regained a measure of her former calm. The family she was working for began to speak highly of her new maturity. They even talked about letting her go at the end of the winter, although with a note of regret that she truly appreciated. Everyone hoped she would stay on in the district, which pleased her even though she forced herself to hide it.

Spring finally arrived after an uneventful winter. Government agents came to inquire after her. From what I heard, she'd become a responsible young woman, and they decided she could be taken off their rolls and could go where she liked. At last, Salomé's life appeared to have a future.

She was, however, indifferent to the praise that was heaped on her. She thought only of the unformed being she had buried under the red oak. If it had been up to her, she would have been like the young man whose situation was talked about in the parish, and whom she secretly admired. He had been found one winter night as an infant wrapped in a burlap bag behind a tavern in Memramcook; two People of the River had forgotten him there after a night of drinking. A local family took pity on him and brought him into their home without even taking the government allowance. The child was raised like their other children, he bore the same name as them and went to the same school. But the mother died, and as soon as he turned sixteen, he returned to the People of the River. Everyone had an opinion about the affair, saying that the lad had no business going back to those people. The young man knew the villagers couldn't understand his decision, but he had to live with his own kind for a while in order to regain the knowledge he felt he was missing out on. After a few years among the People of the River, he left the area and was never heard from again.

That was exactly what Salomé wanted to do: turn her back on all the kindness she had never asked for, return to the People of the Marsh, work out her life apprenticeship among them, and then take to the road for the rest of her life. She often spoke to me about her future during those days when the raspberry tea was having its calming effect on her insides.

When she was just about ready to go, however, she found out that the People of the Marsh had abandoned their native country. Rockport had disappeared, the land completely taken over by the encroaching bush. For a time, she remained where she was, undecided about what to do next.

The answer came from a government agent, a woman who had been widowed early in life and had never had children of her own. Salomé was drawn to her silent sadness. The woman's family was from a parish farther north, near Bouctouche. She had a married cousin whose older children had long ago left home to establish themselves in the city or on their own land, and there was no one living in the house except this cousin, his wife, and a young invalid daughter. As the couple were beginning to get old, they needed someone to help look after things. Would Salomé be interested? Did she want to...? The cousin couldn't pay her much, mind, but all the same... It was a nice district, the agent said, fairly prosperous, lots of big farms, and the people weren't prejudiced against newcomers. It was a good place to start again from square one. The agent told her she would take care of the paperwork, and Salomé would never have to go back to the orphanage. Salomé liked the idea of looking after a young invalid, it appealed to her motherly instincts, and I could feel the waves of euphoria passing through her when she thought about it.

She left a few weeks later, happy to be free and to have somewhere to go. She didn't shed a tear on the day of her departure, which hurt the family she had been living with. But they consoled themselves with the thought that People of the River and People of the Marsh are all the same. They never become attached to anyone.

She almost never thought of that little corner of the world after she left it, except for the tall red oak where she had buried my first incarnation. Every time the tree came to mind, she was gripped by a strong desire to see me, and she would take another look at the men around her, this time a little more boldly than before.

She liked her new place the day she got there. The flatlands sprinkled with wildflowers pleased her, but the best part was that she knew no one and no one knew her.

She liked the family she worked for right from the start. They laughed so much, a person would never know they were as poor as church mice. In his youth, the husband had lived for several years among the People of the Sea, and he retained many fond memories of that time. And he treated Salomé as a member of the family; he teased her about her way of speaking and asked her about the customs in her part of the world, although she herself had begun to forget them. He also appreciated the tisanes Salomé prepared for him. There was one that aided the memory, another that combatted alcoholism, and another that prevented snoring.

For the mother, she made a concoction of birch water and the mushrooms that grew on birch trunks; this healed arthritis and rheumatism. The woman suffered from neither, but she loved the taste of all the medicinal preparations. She was a sweet woman who, though never idle, adored telling sad stories.

The older she grew, the sadder were her stories, and as the years continued to advance, the poorer and more miserable her childhood became.

I remember one evening in July, when we were hulling strawberries on the porch and the heat was turning us all into melting pats of butter, she said to her husband, who pretended to listen to her as he sucked on his unlit pipe:

"Do you remember Mrs. Walker?"

"No."

"Well, she died."

"Ah."

"What about her husband, Mr. Walker? Do you remember him?"

"No."

"Well, he died too."

"Ah, that's too bad."

"He didn't die the same way she did, though. She went into the hospital to have her cancer operated on, and he was going in to visit her. But he had an accident on his way there, and what with all the commotion, he had a heart attack. Then some bandits saw him lying by the side of the road and stole his wallet. Then a Good Samaritan came along and brought him to the hospital, but no one knew who he was because he didn't have his papers on him, so they left him in the hallway on a stretcher. After a while he fell off the stretcher and was lying there on the floor. There were people all around him, and you know what they did? No? Well, they laughed at him. That's when he died. And Mrs. Walker died when she found out about it. It was a darned shame."

"You're right, it was."

Most of the time, the family was happy. They ate well and the house was big enough for Salomé to have her own room, like a princess, with her own key for the door. It was a far cry from the shamelessness of her childhood, where everyone went around naked when the weather was hot. Or her last house, where she had to sneak around to get dressed and undressed without anybody seeing.

This house, on the other hand, had originally been a kind of hotel for itinerant lumbermen. It had at least a dozen bedrooms. The husband's idea had been to make a living from it, but he was a terrible hotelier. He was too fond of chatting with his customers when they came down for breakfast in the morning and came back from work at night. He was their best friend, and he needed all his courage to ask them to pay their bills. Sometimes he forgot to do so on purpose. "These people work so hard," he'd say to his wife, "and they don't make much to begin with. I can't make them do it..." Eventually his wife had persuaded him to stop running the place as a hotel. "At least your clients will stop laughing at you," she'd said. "That'll be something..." And so they were living in a house that was too big for a single family, with a pile of empty rooms that I loved to play in by myself.

The husband and wife liked to call each other "Your Highness" or "Your Majesty." Or else it was "Madame the Marquesa" this and "my dear Baron" that. It was a kind of game played by aging children. The first day Salomé was there, the wife pointed to her husband, who was smoking his pipe in the rocking chair: "Look at His Lordship over there," she said. "Always busy counting his shares and his bonds and his dividends and his cash..." It took Salomé a while to realize that all they had was this huge house and a few acres of land. Salomé played the game along with them. "Are you looking for your comb, Countess?" she'd say. "You probably left it in your jewellery box, beside the Venetian mirror." For the first time in her life, Salomé was content to be like the people around her.

Best of all was the little invalid. Salomé immediately thought of her as a sister. She'd never been close to anyone her own age before, and it seemed to her she had found her first real friend. Which bothered her a little, all the same, because the unfamiliar feelings this aroused in her caused her to forget her resolution to disappear one day on the highways of the world.

The little invalid was exactly Salomé's age, and she returned her affection. She had been like every other girl until the age of eight, always jumping and running everywhere, charming everyone with her innocence and exuberant ways, and all the children in the settlement were her friends. Then one day, for no apparent reason, she began falling down almost every time she took a step. Her legs just gave out from under her, and each time it was harder for her to get back up on her own. No one knew what was wrong. In the end, she lost the use of her legs altogether. The best healers in the region were called in, as well as the priest—even a doctor was consulted—but no one could figure out the cause of her condition. They had to order a wheelchair for her from the city.

The parents in the neighbourhood suspected some kind of contagion, however, and wouldn't let their children play with her. When her brothers and sisters came to visit the house, they avoided kissing and hugging her. She found herself isolated from the rest of the world. Her parents worried about what she would do when they were no longer around. But the young girl never uttered a word of complaint, silently accepting her condition. She was still the same happy girl she'd always been, convinced that surely there must be a cure somewhere in the world.

One day a local woman came by who was well known in the parish for her medical knowledge and the spells she cast on animals belonging to neighbours she didn't like. She examined the girl and declared that she was a woman like any other woman, perfectly capable of bearing children, a diagnosis that made the girl feel much better. Then the old woman took the parents aside and, under strict orders to keep what she was about to say under their hats, told them that if the little invalid successfully conceived a child, she would once again be able to walk. It was a proven cure, she assured them with a wink. The love that a mother feels for her child gives her a strength that no man can possess, and she would have to be able to walk in order to look after her baby, otherwise the child would die, and the young woman had too big a heart to let that happen. The parents thought that that sounded reasonable. All they had to do was find her a husband. "Not necessarily," corrected the old woman, keeping her voice low. "Just a man."

But that was the problem right there. What healthy man would want an invalid for a wife? She might get enough strength back to care for a child, but would there be anything left over for a husband? And a house? She didn't know anything about housekeeping except how to sew, play the harmonium, and sing; she couldn't boil an egg or sweep a floor. It was a rare man they would have to find for her, a saint, and you don't find many of them. Another question, which they never posed aloud: what man would ever be able to feel desire for their invalid daughter?

That was where things stood when Salomé arrived on the scene.

Shortly after her arrival, Salomé began looking for me. She missed her first love more than ever, and thought she saw him everywhere. All the kindness she experienced in her new home increased her impatience and whetted her appetite. She found release only in the caresses she gave herself at night in bed. At first she had to imagine the face of her first love in order to have an orgasm; then, after a while, she had only to remember the smile of the last man she'd met; eventually, she didn't have to think of anyone, her fingers found their way by themselves. From then on, all she needed was herself. She squirmed with greater and greater pleasure, then cried a bit afterwards, finally falling asleep with her face in her hands, which smelled of satisfied desire.

When spring arrived, she went sugaring with the village young-sters. Everyone took part, but not everyone went for the maple syrup candies that attracted the children; most went to drink and carry on like pigs. The adolescents stocked up on white lightning, which they mixed with maple sap, a toxic combination that should be avoided: one drink too many and they got the trots like nobody's business. Or they committed every folly a drunken brain could conceive. Best friends fought with each other until one or both were unconscious. Boys tried to rape their sisters, fathers their daughters, the most straitlaced of wives gave themselves to the first to come along, or even the last to come along. Often it took the rest of the year to live down the shame of sugaring, and only a few had the courage to remember; everyone kept quiet about it because no one was exempt from it. The wiser ones never went back. Some regretted having gone for the rest of their lives.

Salomé was like the others, despite the high opinion she had of herself. She drank moonshine until she lost her judgment, without mixing it with maple sap so as to avoid any intestinal accidents. She was charmed by a tall, young, charmless lout who was already balding and who swore like a trooper. They did it against a maple tree, with their feet in the snow, not even taking off their clothes. Afterwards she fell asleep in the corner of the sugar shack, beside the stove, surrounded by other youngsters who drank, fought, and screwed non-stop all night.

The next morning, she woke up on a straw mattress with a man who smelled of pig shit. He was the local hog butcher, and he never got the smell of pigs out of his skin because he never took a bath. He was one of the few men who didn't drink, so he could take advantage of the women who did. She freed herself from his nauseating embrace and ran outside. The cold air hit her stomach and she vomited up her shame. She'd wet her pants as well, but that didn't bother her too much. She slowly made her way home, exerting all her willpower not to lie down and go to sleep in a snowbank, where she would certainly have been found dead of exposure.

The husband and wife could easily see that she had spent a rough night, but they asked no questions—her breath told the whole story. After all, they themselves had met the same way, in a sugar shack forty years before. They let her clean herself up and wash her clothes, and they gave her some soup and a cup of tea. The next day, she was her old self again.

She went back to work as though nothing had happened, and to make up for her momentary lapse she worked twice as hard as before. For days she toiled like a maniac: she baked bread and made pies, she washed walls and scrubbed floors, she took the little invalid out for walks. She even offered to help out on the farm in order to take some of the burden off the husband, who never asked anyone for help. In short, she wore herself out trying to lose the little life that she believed was growing inside her. She didn't want a son who would grow up to be bald and foul-mouthed. Even less did she want a daughter who would smell of pig shit all her life.

One night, as she was getting ready for bed, she felt her insides churning. She threw on her clothes and ran out into the bush beside the house to rid herself of her little package. The next day, the only trace of her slip in the sugar shack was a fleck of blood on the ground, which she covered with a few shovelfuls of manure. (No wonder I have so few memories of my second incarnation.) After a few weeks she went back to her raspberry tea. She felt sad from time to time, but no more than you'd expect. She remembered the two unknown men too well to feel any remorse. All she retained from the episode was a violent dislike of alcohol and a distinct distaste for young men who lose their hair or smell.

Her desire for a child remained intact, however, and she swore to make the next one with her eyes open, with a man she had chosen. A man who was good for something, not a good-for-nothing.

She kept to herself for a long time after the sugar-shack affair. She never went out with the others on Saturday nights, to dance or drink. Her body was resting.

But nature abhors a vacuum. At the end of the summer, a young woman turned up in the area, a tiny creature who couldn't have been more than thirteen. Her face showed that she had already had a hard life, but she looked intelligent and her expression softened when she thought she was alone. She was an orphan; she'd been auctioned off, but had run away from the farm she'd been sent to. For two years she'd been choosing the dangers of the road over the comforts of servitude. The only clothes she owned were the ones she wore on her back. She didn't even have a pair of shoes; her feet were wrapped up in three pairs of men's thick socks that she wore every day. At the end of the summer she worked the harvest, and when that was over, she gleaned what she could from the fields. Sometimes she performed small chores for the local farmers, cleaning out barns, for example, and was paid with a pint of milk or a crust of bread. She never said thank you, which was a pity because, just looking at her, you wanted to hear the sound of her voice. She knew a few words but preferred using sign language, like someone afraid of giving away too much of herself. No one felt sorry for her — it would have seemed such an insult — and they eventually took her presence for granted, without judging her. She was happy enough to sleep in a hayloft, which she did without asking permission, but also without bothering anyone. Sometimes, if she'd been out too long in the rain, she'd knock on someone's door and ask if she could come in and dry herself off by the stove if she didn't get undressed. That was how, one day, she turned up at the door of Salomé's new house.

By that time, Salomé was feeling so alone that she took to the young woman like a duck to water. The little gleaner reminded her of herself as a young girl, although more courageous than Salomé had been, since this girl had hit the road when she was still a child and didn't have a nickel to her name. Salomé mostly admired her fierce dignity, which also reminded her of her own childhood. She cared for the child as though she found in her an antidote for her own painful memories. Salomé told her that she was always welcome at the house, and the family never asked questions when the child did come back. Sometimes they left food for her on the table, and the little gleaner would take it, but only if no one was watching. One night, when Salomé suggested she take a bath, the child ran off.

It wasn't long before seeing the child again was all Salomé thought about. She even gave her a name, the first one that came to mind, that of a little girl she had known in the orphanage: Andromache. She loved calling her when she saw her coming in the distance: "Andromache! Andromache!

Andromache!" Salomé learned why the child was running loose at such a young age: her mother was an abortionist, and the child had been afraid of becoming pregnant and dying, as her sister had, from a botched abortion. "I was afraid of my mother too," Salomé confided in her one day, but still the little gleaner kept her distance.

Once, overcome by emotion, Salomé tried to kiss Andromache on the mouth, but the child ran away and slept somewhere else that night. Perhaps she was afraid of loving another person. To make amends, the next day Salomé offered her a comb fashioned from a seashell, the kind made by the People of the Marsh, the only keepsake she had from her clan. The child didn't take it, and the next day she disappeared for good.

Her sudden departure hurt Salomé more than she cared to admit. For days on end, she was overcome by fits of tears that made her whole body ache. Uncertain whether her heart was broken by a thwarted friendship or a lost love, she decided the pain caused by the former was as bad as that brought on by the latter. Her misery began to lessen only when she discovered that her comb was also gone. The theft of the comb soothed her, even pleased her. She understood then that she had desired the little gleaner, and could admit to it without shame. In the end, she knew that the child had awakened in her a need for a child of her own, and that her disappearance had left a gaping hole in the middle of her being. It was this new void that was causing her such pain. That winter was the longest Salomé had ever experienced. Maybe the longest in the world.

A young man arrived in the spring whose face seemed familiar. Not as someone Salomé had known before, but as features she had conjured up one night when she was pleasuring herself. He was an itinerant worker who had crossed the entire continent and even once gone to sea. He was exactly the person Salomé had dreamed of: a traveller who wasn't afraid of dropping anchor if he found himself in a place that suited him. He wasn't what you'd call handsome, but he was so kind and easygoing that people were always happy to see him arrive and sorry to see him go. He had a good singing voice, and knew a great many poems and songs that Salomé had never heard before. But his greatest gift was for telling stories — sad and true accounts for women, tall tales for men, moral fables for children. He made up half the details as he went along, for he had a fertile memory. He knew how to read and write, too. What was more, he could use words rather than his fists to silence men who wanted to fight each other when they were drunk or out of work.

The husband of the house was won over immediately. One day he went out to where the young man was working and invited him home for supper, just like that. When the mother saw the young man come into the house, she glanced at her invalid daughter, who had blushed at the thought that this pleasant young man had been invited for her benefit. The mother decided that the two were a perfect match, and the daughter couldn't have agreed more.

At dinnertime, they asked Salomé to eat in the kitchen and serve the family at table—for the first and last time since she had arrived. The mother looked embarrassed when she asked this, but Salomé forgave her willingly. She understood that the invalid's parents wanted to impress the young man with the best they had to offer, and that such opportunities didn't come along every day. They simply wanted this first meeting to go so smoothly that he would want to come back.

Salomé wanted that too. She found him charming. And sharp as a tack. He courted the invalid daughter as though she were every inch the young woman of dignity and station the parents wanted her to be. He knew full well that it was Salomé who had prepared the dinner, but he congratulated the parents and the daughter for the delicious meal. He played the guitar for the daughter, recounted sad but true stories for the mother, and told jokes to the husband. The young man was very good at what he did.

And he set his sights on Salomé. He had undressed her with his eyes the moment he'd entered the house, and she had done the same with him. She knew he wanted her from the way he looked up every time she served him at the table, from soup to dessert. He never spoke a word to her, not even when he was leaving, but he gave her a look that she interpreted correctly: *I'll be waiting for you at my place.*

She waited a while because she was having her period, but

after three days she took him a jug of cold water when he was working in a neighbour's field. She gave water to the other workers too, but spoke only to him. "Where do you live?" she asked him point-blank. "Over there, on the road," he said, pointing to a small wooden caravan that had been pulled there by a mule. Its single window was adorned with a dainty curtain. It was clean inside, and very comfortable, with a small bed and mattress. It was perfect. It was as though their story had already been written by a well-meaning novelist.

The first time she went to him, she simply took him in her arms straight away rather than cozy up to him. She was following a kind of natural impulse that would take an entire lifetime to explain. She knew he was only a boy, that he would never really grow up, let alone be a father to her child. He would remain young and charming forever. His role in life was to please a succession of lovers, and to keep all of them happy.

The family, on the other hand, was convinced that the young man had fallen in love with the little invalid. He was attentive to her at meals, as friendly as you please, and she was obviously in love with him, imagining herself buried by his side for centuries after their deaths. Everything he said was so intelligent, so interesting, so funny. They even forgave him for telling them things they couldn't quite believe — for example, that in cities he'd been in, there were so many people they had to put numbers on the doors of the houses so they could remember where they lived. No one believed him for a minute, but they let him talk on and listened to him politely. He was always invited back, and he always accepted their invitation so he could see Salomé. The only thing he asked was that she be allowed to join them at the table, and the family willingly granted him that favour.

Without wasting any time, the father offered the young man his daughter's hand in marriage. It made perfect sense: he had seen him right off as a son-in-law, which in a way he was. The young man heard him out politely, but turned down his offer. He was an honest man. He wanted to see the world before settling down, he said; he liked to be on the move. He was a citizen of the road. His vocation? To play. "In any case," he said, "my heart belongs to another." (Of course, he was too considerate of the father's feelings to add that by "another" he meant Salomé.) The father said he understood, but he wanted the young man to know that he would be welcome if he ever changed his mind, adding that the big house and farm would be his one day if he married his daughter.

When the husband told his wife that his offer had been turned down, she wasn't discouraged. At least they had tried. And the young man was such good company that he would still be welcome in their house, which pleased the little invalid. Who knew, he might change his mind... The young man continued to spend his evenings at their farm.

The mother was the first to realize that he was visiting their house so often in order to see Salomé. She was slightly annoyed with him for continuing his show of indifference to the servant girl, but she also knew that some battles were lost before they were begun, so there was no point in fighting them.

After the harvest, the young man decided to stay on for a while. He found work at a blacksmith's, where he intended to become an apprentice. He was hoping to be a metalworker when he headed south. Besides, he liked the area, and the people liked him; he was happy there. I liked him too. He was a skirt-chaser like the rest, but he treated his conquests with more respect than the others did.

What Salomé liked about him — she never told him this — was his smell. He'd been born in a lumber camp; his mother had been a laundress and his father drove the company's horses. He'd grown up among lumbermen and began to work in the bush at the age of nine. He'd only left for two years, when he went to school. His long sojourns in the bush had imprinted the indelible scent of wood on his skin. When he ate hare or partridge, which fed on wild herbs, he absorbed their odours and smelled even more like the outdoors. Sometimes he smelled of spruce, sometimes of birch or aspen, depending on the kind of bush he was working in. He also sweetened his breath by chewing spruce gum, so that his mouth never smelled of tobacco. He even brushed his teeth with wood ashes, like the People of the River. His whole body, maybe even his soul, smelled of the bush. Salomé loved his bitter aroma, which for the first time in a long while made her think of the freedom of her childhood.

He and Salomé spent every night in his caravan. The first time, he lit a candle and undressed in its light. She did the same. He caressed her in a way she had never known, and she too invented new ways to please him. They were so happy together, she thought the child he would give her would live a long time because he'd been conceived in such bliss. She also hoped that the little gleaner who had reawakened her desire for a child would be resurrected in her. She would give birth to a girl and call her Andromache. That was what she decided.

One spring morning, despite all the promises the father had

made to the young man to keep him interested in his daughter, the man stopped in front of the house with his mule and his caravan to say goodbye. The parents were sure that the little invalid would cry her eyes out, but she took his departure surprisingly well. She was polite to him, wished him luck in his travels. The previous night he had said his goodbyes to Salomé by making love to her twice. He'd asked her to go with him, but he hadn't insisted. She understood that he was merely asking her out of kindness, and she had said no, thank you, not this time...

Several weeks later, there was great joy in the household: the little invalid was expecting a child! She'd missed her period for two months in a row, and the midwife came and confirmed the news that everyone wanted to hear. The parents were overjoyed, of course, but the father couldn't help thinking bitterly of the young man's hasty departure. Salomé hugged the daughter to congratulate her, but also with a certain reserve.

That same day, the little invalid tried but failed to stand up. "Nothing to worry about," they told her, "you'll be able to walk after your delivery, not before. If what the midwife says is true, no one will be able to call you an invalid after that." Obviously, it would be a bit embarrassing to explain to the people in the parish that the newborn wouldn't have a father, but never mind, they'd deal with that later. The important thing was that the daughter would regain the use of her legs. In any case, it wasn't as if the situation were unusual; theirs was far from the first family this had happened to.

But there came other, less welcome news. One sunny morning, the little invalid decided to play the piano for her unborn child. She thought if she played beautiful music during her pregnancy, her child would grow up to become a musician. But she needed help getting out of her wheelchair, and it was one of Salomé's duties to provide this service, which normally she didn't mind doing because she liked listening to music too.

But this morning Salomé refused. "No," she said coldly, "I can't. I'll strain myself if I try to pick you up." The parents gave her a puzzled look at first. Then, seeing her lower her gaze, comprehension dawned. They sat the girl down in the father's chair, a rare privilege, and asked her straight out...Looking away and swallowing a smile, Salomé said yes. The parents said nothing. They didn't even bother asking her the name of the father; they knew who it was.

For the next few days, Salomé and the little invalid spent a lot of time together, not saying anything, simply reminiscing, and before long they had forgiven each other.

"I don't blame you," the little invalid said to Salomé. "I can't even say I wouldn't have done the same thing if I had been you, because I did do it..."

"I love you so much," declared Salomé, "I could never be jealous of you..."

The two women also forgave their prodigal, faithless lover. Deep in their hearts, they knew he was little more than a child himself, capable of making others like him but incapable of being their father.

I can't say I missed him. Without a father in my life, I was free to choose my own mentors. I had Salomé, and Papa, and the others in the family. All was well. But I admit I would have liked to have heard him sing a song, or tell a story. And I would have liked to smell the bush on his skin.

The parents thought about sending Salomé away, but the little invalid wouldn't hear of it: Salomé was her best friend. So they decided to let Salomé remain in the house at least until she had her baby. After that, they would see. They would ignore the wagging tongues in the parish; and anyway, Salomé was hardly the first servant girl to be put in the family way by an itinerant worker. The only difference was that the young man who smelled of the bush wasn't missed after that; there was no more pining for him to come back. The parents were even relieved that he had gone without telling anyone where he was going.

Life went on as if nothing had happened, except there was a new division of labour among the three women. The little invalid, who until then had swanned around like a princess who couldn't dirty her hands, spending all her time playing parts of tunes on the piano and rereading the three picture books in her possession, discovered that she had a talent for sewing and kitchen work. She took to sleeping on the ground floor, beside the stove, so she wouldn't have to be carried up the steep stairs to her room. The father and mother did more than their usual share of work on the farm and in the kitchen, and all the activity seemed to take twenty years off their ages. They looked after Salomé so solicitously, she stopped taking her salary, so that after a few weeks it was as though they were a family of four, soon to become six.

My half-sister was born two days after me. The house suddenly filled with the cries of babies, but the adults were happy. The only disappointment was that the little invalid, now my aunt, never did regain the use of her legs. The healer woman, who happened to be passing through the region at the time, simply said that the remedy didn't always work, and that maybe it would work later. The parents consoled themselves by saying that at least their daughter was a normal woman, and that she was happier than she'd ever been, which was true. My aunt was sad for a day or two, but soon got over it when she began to play with her daughter.

As for me, I was happy that I could finally see what Salomé looked like. She'd been rubbing her belly and talking to me for nine months. I was born in the henhouse, not the most elegant setting in which to enter the world of the living, but I was in a hurry to get out and didn't give her time to go for help. The man I was to call Papa cut my umbilical cord. I was born like one of the People of the Marsh, with my mother standing up.

It was interesting to see what the world looked like, and I basked in all the light that surrounded me after spending nine months in darkness. I had liked the time I spent inside my mother, but nine months was a bit long. I'd absorbed everything Salomé had told me about the lives of her ancestors. I understood a lot about the world: how it had been formed, what the sky and the stars are made of—the kinds of things we forget later on in life because they aren't essential. I also knew that men and women don't die; they go on living in the dreams we have at night and during the day, and only completely disappear when we forget about them.

But Salomé was disappointed. She'd been expecting her little gleaner, Andromache, and here she was with a tiny boy in her arms. She nursed me for a while, without looking at me, but then she didn't want to have anything to do with me.

Luckily, my aunt had more milk than she knew what to do with, and she took over the task. Then Salomé came to her senses and took me back.

The first time she held me in her arms again, she looked at me as if to ask: Do you know? I said yes as well as I could: yes, I knew about the two others who had come before me. If I had had the words, I could have told her exactly where they were buried, and how. I knew about the People of the Marsh, and the River, and the Sea, who'd been wandering the Earth for three thousand years, and the others who came and went, those who took their places and then were chased off by still others, who would one day be chased off themselves, since that is the history of the world around here; it doesn't do to become attached to any one place. I also knew about little Andromache. Salomé wept with joy: I too had what was a kind of racial memory of our forgotten language. I had existed in spirit for centuries, and now it was time for me to step out into the world.

After several days, I stopped crying. I could smile, look around, move a bit here and there, but that was it. My half-sister cried enough for both of us. My silence worried the woman I called Nanna. Later, when I was about eight or ten months old and she was giving me my bath, she asked me: "How is it that you never cry? You never make a sound, not even when you laugh." Papa, who was smoking his pipe in the same room, spoke almost angrily to her. "Don't talk to him like that," he said. "You'll make him think he's deaf and dumb, and then others will think it too. You have to be careful." He stood up, hid in another part of the room, and called my name. I raised my head and looked around for him. Then, when he appeared at the kitchen door, I smiled at him. Only at him. "You see, he hears everything. He's just a quiet boy, doesn't like to talk, that's all."

"I guess you're right," said Nanna.

"It may just be that he knows a lot of things," said Salomé, "and sometimes it's better not to let on. I think he's just smart." She was secretly delighted that I would never use words to maim or kill, but she couldn't explain that to anyone.

When my half-sister and I celebrated our third birthdays, the doctor came to see my aunt, whom I no longer called the little invalid. While he was there, he asked my mother about my mutism. Salomé was frightened, I remember, and took me in her arms and made to run off with me. The doctor left a few minutes later without charging for his visit.

Of course, I loved my half-sister. She liked that I protected her and I enjoyed being the older brother. When we stopped sleeping in our mothers' beds, we slept together for years. We played together all day, took our meals together, went to the toilet at the same time, had the same childhood diseases, and were never apart for a single day or night. It was as though we'd been married at birth.

But I also liked being on my own once in a while. I'd hide in one of the many empty rooms of the house, or wander off to a distant part of the farm to play with my imaginary friends. Everyone found that cute and left me to make my own decisions.

Papa and Nanna seemed to grow younger and younger each year. They loved Salomé so much, they turned a blind eye to her oddities. She had started taking up with men again, not because she wanted another child but because she missed the pleasures of lovemaking. She liked the amorous glances that slid her way, the rough caresses of impatient men, and she came hard, quickly, and often. (That's what she told my aunt, in any case.) She hung around with the craftsmen and the itinerant workers, turning her nose up at the local men, finding them immature, common, and boring. She also liked the fact that outsiders were discreet and didn't stay long. They were much more considerate than the men around the parish; she would never bother with a man who would boast of having "had her" or used other language that showed his lack of respect. She didn't mind being piggish in bed, but she hated anything vulgar. In her own vocabulary, her sex was her "nest," and when she went out at night, she would say to my aunt that she was going to find "a migrating bird to sleep in my nest." Her phrases were fanciful, but they said all she needed to say. She didn't stay out all night very often, unless it was necessary—she usually managed to be home before dawn—and each time she was out with a man, she was in a good mood for days afterwards. Perhaps that was why Papa and Nanna never said a word to her. They knew she was happy, and understood that she was still a young woman with needs that had to be fulfilled from time to time if she was to stay that way. Papa thought he was the only one who knew when Salomé was out all night, and he said nothing to Nanna for fear of alarming her. But Nanna wasn't blind either, although she said nothing to her husband for fear of upsetting him. The person who was happiest about these nocturnal episodes was my aunt, who loved it when Salomé told her everything that had happened. "What was he like?" And Salomé would tell her, as a way of sharing her pleasure with her friend. Afterwards, my aunt would ask to be left alone for a while, and would close her eyes the better to think about what she had heard.

I was the happiest child in the world when I lived in that house, even though I didn't really belong there. Since that time I have been able to feel perfectly at home anywhere, wherever the kitchen smells of good food: buckwheat pancakes drowning in molasses, baked beans, roast pork, onion omelettes cooked in butter, mince pies. My half-sister and I wore clothes made from the family's hand-me-downs, which Salomé and my aunt miraculously altered to fit us. My half-sister let me play with her doll, and I let her use my fishing rod whenever she wanted it. We never argued, we grew up in total freedom. And the more we grew, the more we pitched in with the housework, taking some of the burden off our grandparents. I know what paradise is: I grew up in one.

My half-sister and I always went to bed early. Lying side by side in our small bed in the room we shared with Salomé, we would hear our grandfather in the next room saying his prayers before going to sleep, which were invariably followed by a string of loud farts that always made us laugh. Sometimes, when my half-sister was sound asleep, I would be awakened by the sound of my mother getting dressed to go out. When she told my aunt about her nocturnal escapades, she would say that she was going out to be a woman; she wanted to reawaken her taste for the future, she said, so she could see it coming. I liked watching the care she took to be as silent as a shadow, but I could never stay awake long enough to see her come back. When she noticed I'd been watching her make her secret preparations, she would blow me a kiss from the door, and I would give her a small wink of encouragement that she couldn't see in the room's darkness.

The only sadness I remember experiencing was when our dog died. He was an English sheepdog that a neighbour had given us to replace the lame kitten we'd had that was picked off by an eagle. The dog was unruly and hard to love, but we spoiled him anyway. We were warned to keep him tied up whenever a pack of coyotes began howling at the edge of the trees, but of course we children wouldn't dream of subjecting him to such a cruel punishment. Coyotes, however, are smart animals, and one of their tricks is to send a female in heat close to the farm when there's a dog on the loose. The female circles around the dog, and the dog, sensing an opportunity to mate, runs after her. She leads him a merry chase, making sure he's exhausted by the time she finally lures him towards her pack. Suddenly the dog finds himself surrounded by a band of coyotes ready to make a meal of him. Sometimes wolves will play the same game. That's how we lost our poor dog, because he didn't know how to control his passions. I had nightmares about it for weeks; I was afraid the same thing would happen to my mother.

Then came the day when a team of workmen arrived in the parish with their heavy machinery. It was quite an event. They were big, hard-working men, charged with the task of building a bridge and repairing all the roads and culverts. They had to be lodged somewhere, and Nanna allowed Papa to reopen the house as a hotel, as it had been before. Suddenly the house was ringing with the sound of many voices, and we children were delighted.

Papa loved to go and watch them work and shoot the breeze, and we gladly went with him. Nanna told the story later to one of her relatives, and I was allowed to listen because they thought I was too young to understand.

Salomé was hired to work as a cook in the construction camp. For the first time in her life she was earning a real wage, and she was proud to wear her chef's hat and apron in the colours of the construction company. In my opinion, she looked ridiculous in the uniform, especially with the chef's hat hiding her beautiful black hair, but she was so pleased with herself that I didn't let her know what I thought. She came back from work every night exhausted but with a dreamy smile that made her look even more beautiful than usual.

Here was the thing: the camp foreman was none other than the young student from Salomé's youth, the first man she had fallen for. He recognized her right away, and even remembered her name. No one had ever paid her such a compliment before.

He was also living at our house. He had the best room, right at the front, the only one with two windows.

He had finished his studies in philosophy and theology, Salomé later told Nanna. (She didn't know what "philosophy" or "theology" meant, but she pronounced the words as though she'd been saying them all her life.) At the last minute he had turned down the ministry he'd been offered; he longed to work with his hands, like his forebears. He had therefore gone to work for this construction company, which belonged to the father of a friend of his. His parents had been against it, of course, but they had probably been consoled by the idea that this was another thorn they could add to the crown that had long dignified the family name.

He had started out in the accounting office, but asked to be switched to working outside. After learning several trades, he had been made foreman. As he was educated and yet respected his fellow workers who were not, he had been given additional responsibilities. He had become the boss of the camp, and before long the company had him working in the towns; his apprenticeship in the field was over. According to Salomé, who told me all this while bathing me, his men liked his educated way of speaking; listening to him made them feel as intelligent as he was. He didn't mind their rough words and their enormous capacity for beer, but he made them behave respectfully towards the people who lived in the towns they were working in, especially the women. Tears filled her eyes as she related these marvels, and I suspected her of inventing things she didn't know.

It was obvious that Salomé had fallen for him all over again —even I could see that. In her heart she convinced herself that he had left his well-to-do family in order to lead the kind of life she had dreamed of. It wasn't true, she knew that better than anyone, but she forced herself to believe it. Soon she was spending the whole night in his room, no longer even coming into our room to change before disappearing until morning. They'd sit out on the veranda with us after supper then go upstairs to his room, hand in hand, like a young married couple.

He was the one she left me for.

I still can't be angry with her, because I loved both of them. It was in her nature to do what she did, and no force on earth could have prevented her from doing it. She absolutely had to go back and repair her broken childhood. I still remember him, his large grey eyes that always seemed to be looking into his own dreams, his blond curls wet with sweat, his face baked by the sun. He was forever covered with dust, but he never looked dirty. He was kind to me. I've never been able to hold a grudge against him, because all he wanted was to make my mother happy for a while. Another thing: I loved hearing him talk, and it was through him that I learned how to articulate my own thoughts and dreams. It was as though he'd given me the power of speech—a precious gift that helped me live a life of solitude.

I remember Salomé hiding her carpet bag behind the stable, me following her and the two of us laughing like a couple of accomplices playing a good joke on someone.

When the men finished their work in our region, they broke camp after spending the whole night celebrating. I was at the party with Salomé, Papa, Nanna, my aunt, and my half-sister. It was fun. Everyone had a lot to drink and eat, there was singing and dancing and laughing. You'd have thought it was Salomé's wedding they were celebrating, she was so happy to have finally reconnected with her childhood sweetheart, and she was friendly to each of the guests in turn, as though she were a queen greeting her subjects. She and I were the only ones who knew. In fact, as I learned later from Nanna, not even the camp foreman knew that she intended to follow him for the rest of his days. His company had offered him an important project in town, and Salomé's plan was to move there without talking it over with him first.

I still wonder what he must have thought when, the next day, as the men were packing their equipment, he looked up and saw Salomé with her carpet bag and her walking stick, wearing her chef's hat, asking what vehicle she was assigned to, as though she were a permanent member of the team. All I know is that she left.

Papa and Nanna didn't say anything for a few days; neither did my aunt. I didn't cry, but for several weeks I went around with a pained expression on my face. I knew in my heart that she was never coming back, but I would have liked someone to say something, so that I wouldn't have had to think about it so hard. I looked all around the house for her, in the sheds, in the fields, hoping I was wrong. I waited for her at night at the farm gate, afraid that Papa and Nanna would be angry with her because she'd gone out without telling them, and I was ready to defend her against their reproaches. I followed my grandparents' eyes, thinking they knew where she was hiding. Then, tired of waiting and looking, I sat beside my aunt's wheelchair and she stroked my hair, heaving long, heavy sighs.

Finally, Papa took me aside and told me that Salomé had met a man who loved her and whom she loved too. He didn't know if or when she would come back. "Think of her, because she loves you too, and hope that nothing bad happens to her," he said. "There was no life for her here, with her health the way it was. She needed to see the country, and more of the world than just us. She left you with us because she loves you and because she loves us." After that explanation, which sounded to me a bit forced, not that I minded, I began to feel less pain, and stopped looking for her, although I thought of her all the time. It was as though she'd gone to heaven without dying. I didn't worry about her being eaten by ravenous coyotes, which was a good thing. I know now that she sent us money for a while, and even a letter once, that someone wrote for her but which no one read to me. That was about it.

My only sadness came from the sadness of others—from Nanna and my aunt, who cried for a long time. Their suffering made me feel ashamed, and even though I was proud to see that Salomé was so loved, I was angry with her for causing them such sorrow. But I had to forgive her—she was the soul, heart, head, and even the body of our house; we did nothing without her, she filled it with life. I would die too if I was angry with her. Maybe forgiving her was selfish, but it was the sword that protected her from others, and the shield that guarded me from my own poisonous resentment. That's probably why I've been so quick to forgive others in my life: I could disarm those who wanted to do me harm, and ward off the hatred I might have had for myself. It's also why I avoided harming others: I didn't want to have to rely on their forgiveness.

But what I missed most was the bond that the two of us had formed since my birth. I was her only real companion, the one who shared her bed, the one she confided her secrets to in words she reserved for grown-ups. That time was over. I transferred my affections to my half-sister, who didn't respond as well because she had already formed a similar bond with my aunt. That place was taken, and there were a few hard feelings for a while. But in the end, that too passed.

What was harder to get over was watching Nanna die. In her case, her leaving us was so long in coming, and so final, that I was heartbroken for a long time. The house no longer smelled of bread and cookies fresh out of the oven, and I was afraid I would die of hunger. I took to hiding heels of bread here and there around the house, telling myself that at least one of us would survive. When my half-sister found out, she scolded me for the first time in her life. I remember that I wasn't very proud of myself, and I never did it again.

I also remember thinking that Salomé had been right to leave us, so that I could miss her even more. Ours had become a sad house, like the houses in the stories that Nanna so liked to read. My aunt stopped playing the piano, she and my half-sister cried all the time, and Papa mostly went around looking lost. Without the help of our neighbours, who regularly brought us meals, we would have starved.

That winter seemed particularly long and hard. Luckily, Papa's three other daughters came to visit from time to time. Each of them stayed for a few weeks, and together they managed to get the household back on track.

My half-sister was the next one to go. My aunt's condition was deteriorating day by day, she could no longer look after her daughter, she felt her end drawing near and began talking about going to join Nanna. It was she who asked her favourite sister to take the little one.

One spring day, the sister arrived with a small suitcase and the kind of doll that was sold in big department stores in the city, not the kind that were made at home out of bits of wood and rags and painted all sorts of different colours. I gathered the idea was to pacify my half-sister, and she was so delighted with it that she named it Salomé and promised to love it forever as long as it didn't go away. My half-sister left with her new mother so quickly, I wasn't even aware she was going until she was gone. I was so stunned by her disappearance that it never occurred to me to go looking for her.

I saw her again years later, when I got out of the asylum. She'd been well taken care of. Her second mother had put her through school, then let her take a hairdresser's course so she could get a job in the city and send money back to her adoptive family. There she met a young man who married her even before she was pregnant. Her husband was a worker and was gone for months at a time; he came back with piles of money, enough for the family to live on for a year, and when the money ran out, he went back to earn more. A common-enough story in these parts. She liked telling her new family about her happy memories of our childhood together. I was a kind of hero to her children, their mother's loyal little companion. But we didn't meet up again in the coming years; I'd only been passing through, and I think she's dead now.

My aunt didn't stay with us for long either. One day an ambulance came for her, and she was taken to a sanitorium in Edmundston, I think it was — in any case, somewhere too far away for us to visit her. I don't know when she died, to be honest, but I'm told it wasn't long after that. Papa cried for her when she was far from us, but after he found out she was dead, he stopped crying. He said he didn't have the strength to keep it up anymore.

That left just me. Mentally, I'd already begun to pack my bags; I threw in all the essentials, and added or subtracted things as they occurred to me. I'm never so distracted that I forget to think about the present. That's been the story of my life: I'm always preparing for the next big journey so that I won't be taken off guard by present events. The only time I didn't do that was when I was in prison or the asylum, and even then I was always off somewhere in my head.

Still, Papa made sure I would be taken care of. He decided to ask one of his sons, who lived up north somewhere and had worked all his life but never owned his own home, to come and live with us. He wasn't a very friendly man, he had a voice like someone who never washed his hands — or brushed his teeth, either. He didn't like to see Papa rocking me to sleep at night because I wasn't one of the family. Whenever I climbed up on Papa's lap, he told me to get down, and Papa had to look at him sternly to get him to back off.

The bargain they struck, as far as I could tell from their conversations, was that the son got the land and the house in exchange for housing and feeding Papa for the rest of his life. The son and his wife had plenty of children, and the son planned on taking in a lot of pensioners in order to make a bit of money off them. So there was no place for me. The son spoke often about the orphanage, and the very word terrified me. I knew a lot of people who'd gone to that institution. Some of them were very well treated, others not so well, but the one thing I was certain of was that I would never go there myself, out of respect for my mother. Besides, I wasn't an orphan: I knew who my mother was, I remembered my father, the man who smelled of the bush and who might still have been alive. I had Papa and my half-sister, I was not alone in the world. I wouldn't let anyone say I was an orphan.

The other option was the children's auction in Bouctouche. I think Papa wanted to take me there himself rather than risk his son throwing me out onto the street or sending me to the orphanage, which he would have done at the drop of a hat. "Salomé's bastard," he used to call me, pleasant charmer that he was. There was no place for me under his roof: "I wasn't brought into this world to look after someone else's brat." He said the auction was a more humane solution, and less painful for Papa, who'd ended up loving me in spite of himself. As I loved him. He was all I had left of Salomé in this world.

I don't like to think of my final days in the house on the hill. The son's family had already moved in, and for several days I'd been sleeping on a straw mattress beside the stove, which it was my job to light in the morning and keep going all day. The son's wife said it was good training for my future life as a domestic. The children were kind to me, even though their father scowled at them whenever they smiled or put in a good word for me. His wife, who wasn't afraid of him, became very generous towards me when she realized I was going. She even gave me her eldest son's first Communion suit so that I would look spiffy at the auction.

The morning of my departure, she showed me how to brush my teeth and gave me one of her old toothbrushes. She made me take a bath; she even washed my hair and sprinkled in some hair lotion that belonged to her husband, telling me that it could be a little secret between us. Then she showed me what I looked like in a pocket mirror she had. "You're handsome," she said. "You'll go with the first round, and for a lot of money, too." She was in a hurry to see me go, but she went to a lot of trouble. The thought gave me some self-confidence: I didn't feel chased out of the house, only ushered out by a necessity greater than myself.

Finally, she let me eat by myself at the table while the other children, who'd already had their breakfast, were outside playing in the snow. She served me as if I were a special guest: eggs, sausages, pancakes drenched in maple syrup and cream. "Eat up, boy," she kept saying. "It's going to be a long day. You have to build up your strength."

I put on my coat, which had belonged to my aunt when she was little, my woollen toque, my mitts, which weren't the same colour, and my boots. When I was dressed, I picked up my little suitcase, which was almost empty — there was only a change of underwear and a broken toy that my half-sister had forgotten on purpose so I would have it, and a lead soldier that I had been given permission to take — and she gave me a friendly pat on the head: "Go now, they're waiting. And good luck, boy!" I understood that my leaving was final because of the suitcase she'd given me, but I had no idea where I would end up.

The son was waiting in the buggy he'd hitched up, and Papa was pacing around, smoking his pipe and talking to himself. I could see he was in a foul mood. The son gave the signal to the horses. The snow had stopped and it was raining, but at least it wasn't as cold as it had been even a few minutes before.

The few memories I have of that day are shrouded in a confusion that I actually found comforting. When we were two miles from Bouctouche, Papa told his son to stop; we would go the rest of the way on foot, Papa and I. He told me to get down, and then he jumped down behind me. The son grumbled. Papa told him to turn around and go home, he would ask a neighbour to bring him home after the auction. "Come on, Dad, be reasonable!" But Papa repeated his order in a drier tone. I was glad to be alone with him. Suddenly I felt like his favourite, and his son's displeasure made it even better. I didn't even look at him when he left.

We walked hand in hand for a while, then he let go of mine to light his pipe. He stood between two spruce trees beside the road, but he still had a hard time of it; the lighter didn't work well in the cold. When he finally got his pipe lit and had taken a few puffs, he began to talk. It was as though he were still talking to himself and didn't quite want me to hear what he was saying.

"A man can't always do what he wants to in life, you know, especially when he's still a kid. And it's even worse when he's old. I don't make the decisions in my own house anymore. It's not even my own house now. So that's why we're going today to find you a new home. You'll be better off there than you would be staying with me, especially after I'm dead. You'll make friends, you'll learn different things. The rest of us, especially me, we'll be thinking of you and hoping nothing bad happens to you. And if anything of that nature does come your way, just think about your poor old dead grandmother's face, and all your troubles will take themselves off on their own. That's what we call 'calling on the souls of the dead.' The People of the Marsh do that, and that's where your mother came from. Also think of those who love you — that's good too: your mother, your half-sister…" It started raining harder at that point, and his pipe went out. I would have tried to comfort him, but I didn't know how.

Before we got to the village, he stopped to take a sip from the flask of homemade blueberry alcohol he carried. When we arrived at the manse beside the church, the government agent was waiting for us. He was wearing a three-piece suit. He offered Papa a cup of tea and me a cup of hot chocolate, which we gladly accepted. He left us to ourselves to rest a little, and Papa said to me, "I'm going to watch the auction from the back of the church to make sure you leave with a good family." He was crying hard, and I could barely see him, and I almost wished he would just go.

I can still see him stand up, wipe the tears off his face with his sleeve, and kiss me on the mouth. I liked the way his breath smelled of alcohol and tobacco. Then he turned and left the church, walking slowly, like a man climbing a scaffold.

Through the frost-covered church window, I tried to follow his movements, to see where he was going, but it was no use. He quickly disappeared into the fog.

PART SIX

And now the merry-go-round has started up again, as you might say.

My adoptive family seems to have found peace again. Last night we had an excellent dinner; I even took two helpings, like the first time I was sold at auction. There was spruce beer and dandelion wine, and several toasts were proposed even though our hearts weren't in it.

Early this morning, after breakfast, the wife made everyone leave the house so I could have a quiet bath in the kitchen. She pressed my suit and shirt. She combed my hair and tied the knot in my tie for me, since I still haven't learned how to do it myself. When I was ready, the family came back in. We were all a little ill at ease, like people who've just been told an embarrassing truth.

By way of taking our minds off things, I handed out the little treasures I've been saving during my time here. An alarm clock that works like new, since I've never once used it; they probably won't use it either, because their children wake them up every morning, but it will look good on their dresser, and it will keep time if they wind it up properly. To the children I gave my deck of cards, my dice, and a nickel for each of them so they can buy some penny candies at the general store. I gave my lead soldier to the youngest; it had stayed with me all these years. The little one jumped for joy, as I recall. He began playing with it and broke it—not seriously. I could have fixed it in a minute, but I didn't have the time.

I took nothing with me but my little suitcase containing a change of underclothes, my toothbrush, and my shaving kit. I'll also have my watch and the money I've earned since coming here, and on my finger the signet ring given to me by the woman I loved; I can always pawn it if I get hard up. Everything else is in a large cloth bag that I've hidden beside the river in case the auction turns out badly.

I've also decided to leave them my book of stories. The children will be able to get the same amount of pleasure out of it that I did, if they ever learn to read. As for the stories, I'll be carrying them around in my head. They'll be safe there.

I've been thinking about the woman I loved for several days now. Whether that's a good or a bad sign, I don't know.

She's dead. Exactly when she died, I can't say anymore. I'm having a hard time keeping track of the years, especially the more recent ones.

Before knowing her, I'd had a long and happy youth. It was as though I'd been twenty years old for twenty years. I moved around a lot. Salomé would have been proud of me. I sailed with the fishing fleet for a time, and went as far as that would take me. I spent a lot of time in the bush, too, working as a lumberjack and a cook, and for a few years I smelled strongly of the bush, like the man who made me.

I admit that I often thought about looking for Salomé, but I didn't really try all that hard; the idea of seeing her again bothered and appealed to me at the same time. For a while I lived near Néguac with some People of the River who were related to us. I worked with them as a smuggler, although that's a word they don't like to use; they prefer the term "commercial traveller." A few of them remembered her, others had heard her name, but I learned nothing useful for a long time. Someone told me one day that she'd lived all over the Maritime provinces, with a lot of different men; she had children with two of them, but no one knew what became of them. Someone else told me that one day, when she was sick, some nuns who once ran a leper colony in Tracadie took her in. She didn't have leprosy, but she wasn't in good shape. She'd been ravaged by an assortment of maladies, she was starving to death, she'd lost all her hair and her teeth. But she got better in the end, and worked for several years at the convent to pay them back for their charity. She died there. The year I must have turned thirty, I decided I'd had enough of such legends; none of them sounded right to me. I packed my little bag and set off to find her myself.

I had no trouble finding the former leper colony; there'd only been one in the province. The nuns had converted it into a small hospital that also served as a school for young girls. One night I showed up at the door, and I guess I must have looked like a beggar because they let me in and gave me something to eat. I remember the macaroni because it was the first time I'd ever had it, and I liked it so much I've never wanted to eat it anywhere else. I was given a corner to sleep in, and in the morning they told me I could stay for a few days and have my meals in exchange for some work. There was a stone wall they wanted built, and they had no one else to build it. In the end, I stayed there for a few months.

I looked everywhere for signs that she'd been there. I should have looked in the cemetery, but that was the last place I thought of. I was fortunate enough to make friends with a good nun who was a kind of prophetess, but the kind you never listen to unless you've suffered in life, which was in fact my case. One morning when winter had almost arrived at our doorstep and the icy wind painted the grass white between the gravestones, she took it into her head to read the names of the people buried there to me. On a rusty iron cross, she read her name. I dropped to my knees. "Yes, this is Salomé," she said. "The Voyager, they called her. Did you know her?" She waited a long time without saying anything, then uttered the words I'd been longing to hear for years. "She spoke of you often. She liked to tell us that your father smelled of spruce trees and that you were born in a henhouse. She loved a great many people in her life, but no one more than you." She took me by the arm and brought me inside because the snow was beginning to fall heavily. Every night of my last week there, she talked about her. It had been a long time since I'd felt so happy, so complete. Suddenly the rage that so often tore through my body vanished. I loved Salomé again, the Salomé I had known, and as she had let herself be known to others. According to my calculations, she died around the time I'd been called the little hireling. All these years I've been in love with a dead woman.

The night when winter arrived for good and a foot of snow blew in from the sea, I set up my tent in front of the rusted iron cross and slept on top of her in the storm. In the morning, I gathered up my things and gave the sisters what little money I had to thank them for taking her in. The prophetess said it wasn't necessary, but I insisted. Finally, she said, "Your mother found her name in the cemetery of our orphanage in Grande-Digue. She took it from there and brought it here, to return it to us. Like a debt she was finally settling. She was an honourable woman. On the way, she made a man of you."

She gave me her last words of advice: "Be careful — don't go looking for happiness. Happiness will wear you out in the long run, and it never lasts. It's physically impossible. You eventually realize you've spent your life in fear of losing it. It's a waste of time, I tell you. Look for contentment instead, it's much more rewarding. And don't make a fuss about life's little troubles. They keep the mind alive, and they stop you from doing something stupid."

I should have listened to her, but all my life I'd been avoiding trouble, and I'd managed it so well that when bad luck did befall me, I was like a declawed cat dropped into a dog-filled alley.

Ten years later, I heard tell of a government program to encourage people to settle the province's deserted coastal areas. A person could get a free plot of land up near Shippagan by agreeing to build a house on it and farm it for a few years. It sounded like a good idea to me. I'd never had any property that belonged to me alone, and I'd always wanted to be a landowner. It would make a nice change, being almost a normal person. The government would also provide funds for buying tools and seeds. With what I had set aside while I was working as a fisherman, I decided I would build myself a house exactly like the one I'd lived in with Papa and Nanna, only smaller. I would make myself a new life, in the true sense of the term.

I ended up in a settlement that still had several plots available—not the best land, but still. The area had been cleared more than a century before, but the land had since been reclaimed by the bush. But because of the earlier settlement, it wouldn't be as hard to clear as virgin forest would have been. There were all sorts of people there. No one knew anyone else, but we all got along well just the same.

I began by building my house, thinking I'd get around to clearing and cultivating the land later. I admit that I never really got around to it, except for putting in a small blueberry patch and a kitchen garden. That was because, as soon as I began constructing the house, my neighbours came by to lend me a hand and word got out that I was a carpenter. Not that I was unusually gifted in that trade, but I took time to think through what had to be done, and used the right tools to do it. I soon had a half cellar for a foundation and a nice little two-storey wooden house, which I painted in bright colours. It was the only house in the settlement that looked like a real house from the outside. The inside was fairly plain, as though it was built for a hermit. I would have liked to have finished it, but I was too busy lending myself out to neighbours who were building their own places and paid me a small fee to help them.

As for women, I was off them. I was no longer the itinerant lover contenting himself with women that other men no longer wanted. I would have liked to have forgotten those sentimental years of my life, but whenever I tried, I couldn't do it. If my life were a novel, those would be the first pages I'd tear out.

My first was a woman with six children, and she was still under thirty. Her husband had left her with nothing for a younger woman. She was facing starvation and was afraid, for good reason, that the government was going to take her children from her. She needed help, and her own family would have nothing to do with her.

One day I found myself standing in front of her house with a map in my hand. I wanted to get to the next village, Petit-Rocher, where I'd never been before, and I needed someone who could read the map. I remember there was a gang of kids playing in the front yard. They looked at me frankly, as though they knew I would never do them any harm, and the woman was kind enough to invite me in. The inside of her house was neat and clean, with no smell of cooking—it smelled more like vacancy and want. She spent a long time studying the map, and I thought for a moment she didn't know how to read, but I soon saw that she was taking her time because she was happy to have some company, it didn't matter who it was, a human being, a man to speak to so she could forget her own troubles for a while.

I had some food in my seaman's bag: a dried sausage, a brick of cheese, some bread, and a chocolate bar. When the children came in one by one from the rain, I took out my provisions and spread them on the table, despite the feeble protests from their mother. I could never resist seeing a child satisfy his hunger, and they were all there looking at me, too polite and well brought up to ask what the deal was, except for the youngest, who pointed at the chocolate bar and asked me what it was; the others blushed on his behalf. I took out my knife and sliced the bread, and cut the sausage and cheese into equal pieces, and invited everyone to the feast. The children asked their mother for permission to accept my offer. She could hardly refuse, seeing how badly they wanted to dive in, and she said yes to reward their good manners. Everything was eaten in an instant—there wasn't a crumb left for the mother.

She smiled anyway. She was happy to see her children happy, even though she knew it couldn't last. She offered me a glass of water, and I showed her the single teabag I had left. She got up to put the kettle on. "It's getting late," she said. "You can stay the night if you want. I can make up a bed for you on the floor in the kitchen. I'm afraid that's the best I can do. We don't get many visitors here. But at least you can rest for a while before you leave." The children begged me to say yes. "Stay, mister, stay!" I couldn't refuse; I wanted to be wanted.

The next morning, I took the two oldest children to the general store and bought enough provisions for a week. There was a bit of flour left in the pantry, and some winter apples in the cellar, some milk and molasses. I remember her making me an omelette so huge it made me want to fall in love with her. There was work in the region; the harvest had just begun. I could stay with her, she said, if I paid for my keep with food. I quickly forgot about going to Petit-Rocher.

It took her a while to join me on the kitchen floor. The first time I entered her, she came almost immediately and looked at me for a long time with tears in her eyes. After a week, her daughters told her to take me into her own bed. "It must be hard," said her youngest, "lying on the floor like that, the poor man," and the eldest daughter blushed. At night, before and after making love, she would whisper, "Please, stay here, don't go now…" Her need touched me deeply. She didn't love me, I knew that, but she needed me, and that was enough.

I found work, and the money began coming in. With the garden, some fishing, and the deer that a neighbour shot for us in the fall, we had more than enough to see us through the winter. We even bought shoes for the children, and the bank no longer threatened to seize the house and land. The woman told me every day that she loved me, that she'd never loved anyone but me, and of course I pretended to believe her. And I have to admit I was happy living in that house: I was a hero to the little ones and a godsend to their mother. I would have liked to be loved for myself, but I could get along without that.

In the spring, the old wanderlust took hold of me again. I knew I'd be hired on one of the fishing boats in a second. She didn't say anything when she saw me packing my bag. She'd begun taking in sewing from the women in the area, and her two oldest daughters were working on a neighbouring farm; she didn't need me as much anymore. She didn't beg me to stay. What woman in her right mind would want to share her life with a dumb poet?

When I came back in the fall, my place had been taken by a distant cousin, a nice guy who was good with the children. I was introduced as a "former boarder," but he was too smart to be fooled by that. She was an honest woman, and she insisted on giving me back all the money I'd sent her when I was away. I didn't stay long, not even a night. When she walked me down to the gate, she kissed me and said, "Thank you for having been a part of my life. You saved us. You'll find happiness somewhere else. I'm sure another woman will need you." "You're right," I thought. "I'll run into another woman who will need me. Once again I'll be the knight in shining armour, and I'll be loved by some poor chatelaine who's been treated unjustly by her lover. That's my role in life." I left with a heavy heart all the same.

I spent the winter with another woman, but I left in the spring because her children had been badly brought up. They treated me like a hero too, but life there was simply too hard. I could do better. She cried a lot, she said her world had come to an end, she didn't want to go on living and ended up sending me off with curses. "Now I'll have to find someone else," she moaned. I couldn't get out of there fast enough. Three weeks later, I had found another mother in distress.

The dance of convenient love, in which the predator—awaited, wanted, wished for—embraces his consenting, grateful prey. The music is always the same; the lyrics don't change either, when there are any. Whenever I found myself with a woman who hadn't been able to find anyone better than me, she passed me off as her hired hand. That saved me from trouble with the locals, and from the wagging tongues that flapped like flags in the wind at first but soon settled down. "She wouldn't take him into her bed, surely," they'd say. "Surely not him!" In that way I was following my career as a hired man with a great many fallen women, a career I had learned very young—after my first auction, in fact.

I don't know how many women I saved like that. Six or seven, at least. And a couple dozen children. Of course, I enjoyed staying put for a while with a woman, but the lure of a new one always pulled me away. I like only happy beginnings.

I liked the children too. I played with them as if I were a child myself, I spoiled them, and I came to think that by treating them the way they deserved to be treated, I was erasing the bad memories of the father who had abandoned them. I felt as though I were fixing something that had been broken in them. They loved the pantomimes I improvised for them; they always asked for them. "Sir, do the bear hunt for us!" "Sir, do the thief with the heart of gold!" It didn't take much to make them happy.

Now that I think of it, there was a bit of Salomé in all of that. We missed her so much that she had swollen in our memories, and maybe even taken up more space than she should have. And so I learned from her to trigger this longing. In the end, I perceived a gap in this long scar we call memory, in which are hidden most of our images and recollections of happiness. The gap can close by itself in hard times and reopen in better times. I came to want to live in this gap forever. I wanted to be missed by others the way I missed her.

There was also a bit of me in it. Back when I was the little hireling, I desired all the women who had an advantage over me. Not to take revenge on them for some affront—they never did me any harm, and as a general rule were good people—but to be on the same footing as them. The hired hand as lover threatened the established order, and this thought gave me all my self-esteem.

When I joined the settlement, however, I was certain that that part of my life was over. I was almost forty, and I could no longer be the perpetual son I had been. On the contrary, I finally felt that I was a grown-up. I was settled, I worked as a carpenter in the winter and fished when the fishing was good. I saw women only when I was in port. But still...

There was no one in charge of the settlement as such, except for a kind of government lackey who did a bit of everything; he was the land agent, the municipal clerk, the justice of the peace. For short, we called him the federal agent. His wife taught at the only school in the district, which wasn't very well attended because people had to pay taxes to send their children to it. Either the locals were too poor to pay or else they flat out refused to fork over the money. But she had a good heart, and never made the children pay who found the courage to turn up for classes.

She also sang in the church choir. One day I went there to take care of some odd job the priest had asked me to do, and she was there, standing by the altar beside a woman sitting at the harmonium. They were rehearsing. I didn't dare make any noise with my tools, so I sat down to listen, intending to do the work when they were finished. They gave me a private recital. The acoustics in the church were excellent, and it was as though the woman's voice lifted the little wooden church out of its desperation. She was aware of my presence immediately, and looked me straight in the eye. She knew she had me in her clutches. I fled as soon as I could, and never did go back to do the job; I would have thought about her the whole time, and the work would have suffered for it. The next week I went back on the boats, feeling calm. But after that day, I thought of her as the woman I loved.

I got to know her husband first. I had returned from fishing, and he came over to my house to get me to fill out some form or other. When I'd given him the information, he hung around for a bit, as though looking for something but not knowing what. I had made some coffee and offered him a cup. It seemed to give him the excuse he was waiting for. He asked me in a joking manner if I had something stronger than coffee in the house. I didn't fall for it; I knew full well that the government didn't allow us to have alcohol in the settlement, the whole parish was dry, and I could have been thrown out if they found any liquor in my house. I pretended I was deaf. In the end he left, but not without saying he'd be back.

He returned the next day. He was more forthright this time, asking me point-blank if I was trafficking in alcohol. I shook my head. I did have my own stash, for bringing with me on the boats, but I never sold any. He started to threaten me, subtly at first and then more openly. As the federal agent, he had the power to revoke my property rights if I was too slow in clearing my land. I responded by standing up and looking busy. He left in a fury.

His next tactic was fairly predictable. He came back in a pitiable state. He was falling to pieces, and I decided to take advantage of his condition to get on his good side. As he confessed his weakness for alcohol, I slipped a drop of brandy into his coffee. As soon as he tasted it, he became more talkative and treated me to a rigmarole that made him even more pitiful. He was badly paid, there was no future for him here, he'd been promised a post in Ottawa, but... His wife didn't allow him to touch alcohol because of his health... He never went overboard with it, just a little drink from time to time, to make life seem more worth living... He had no friends in the settlement he could confide in, they were all afraid of him... His children from a former marriage didn't want to see him... A little drink once in a while didn't hurt anyone... We only have one life, after all... I offered him another coffee, which he accepted with enthusiasm, and this time I didn't stint on the brandy.

He knocked it back like a gourmand and stood up. "You, sir, are a gentleman and a true friend. As long as I live, you will have nothing to fear from the government." As for that, I had had some reason to be worried: in the four years I'd been there, I had let my property go uncleared, and if that went on too long, the government had the right to take it back from me. Deep down, I had absolutely no interest in farming; growing crops wasn't my true calling. I just wanted a place of my own, and I liked my house, roughly built as it was, with its back turned to the bush. What I liked best was seeing the bears come out in the fall to help themselves to my wild apples in broad daylight, or the moose that pressed its muzzle up against my window in the mornings. But now, it seemed, thanks to a few drops of brandy, I could relax on that front.

The next week, I slipped a flask of rum into his hand so that he could spike his own coffee from then on. The man left with tears in his eyes. He was entirely won over. I knew it wouldn't be long before he offered me money for booze, and when that day came, I showed him firmly to the door. He came back the next day and begged me to forgive his betrayal of our lasting friendship.

When I had to leave again to go back on the boats, he took me in his arms and begged me not to forget him.

The strange part of it is that he and I ended up sharing a sort of friendship. Each time he came for another of his little refills, he felt he had to favour me with new confidences in order to keep our friendship in balance. I learned that he was on his second marriage. When his first wife died, he'd left his children with his sister-in-law and married the schoolteacher with the voice of an angel after courting her for a long time. She finally agreed to marry him because she believed he was about to be posted to the capital, where she saw herself living the life of luxury she thought was her due. But the promotion never came, and he suspected his wife held it against him personally. To pass the time, she had begun teaching at the school again. He'd given up drinking to please her, and he admitted that that had been the hardest thing he'd ever done. He never referred to her as "my wife," preferring to call her "the woman who sings in church," which I found off-putting, but I didn't mind learning that his marriage wasn't an entirely happy one.

One evening, while I was making tar in my workshop, there came a knock on my door. It was her. As soon as she came in, I realized I'd been waiting for this moment ever since I first saw her. For a moment, I almost didn't recognize her. I remembered her wearing a little green dress with a white collar, and the dainty shoes she'd had on in church, and I'd never really seen her dressed differently. This time she was wearing something more sporty. It suited her, but at the same time it made her look less attractive than she'd been the first time. She'd come by foot and I could see that she was cold.

Without even taking the time to sit down, she said: "It appears to be you who is selling my husband alcohol. Is that true?" I'd never sold him a drop, but I held my tongue. "He's going to kill himself if he keeps drinking. He gets out of his mind when he drinks. It's because of alcohol that we don't have children. It's because of alcohol that we have almost nothing. It's his drinking that has cost him his promotion. Please, stop what you're doing. For my sake." After a moment she agreed to take a chair at my table, and she began to speak of other things. It was good, seeing her there, even if she was too beautiful

258

for me, with her Madonna-like face. I'd always thought that beautiful, blue-eyed blondes existed only in picture books.

When her husband came by for his usual ration, I gave him to understand that he would get no more alcohol from me, it was over. (I did it for her, but I was fairly certain he wouldn't understand that.) He left in a towering rage: "You'll pay for this, you bastard!"

I wasn't sure what to think when she came back. Maybe she wanted to thank me. The pleasure I showed in her company must have moved her, because her visits soon became regular. She never failed to stop by on Sunday afternoons, after Mass, and on Tuesday evenings, and Saturday mornings. I began working on the cabin's interior solely so that it would be more welcoming for her. I didn't have time to finish it, but at least I tried.

Sometimes she dropped by unexpectedly. She would sit in my kitchen, across the table from me, and not say anything, then leave without having so much as opened her mouth. As though she were trying to be like me. In fact, it was because she couldn't make up her mind—or rather, she told me later, because she preferred not to make up her mind. She told me how, as a young woman, she had been courted by two men. Both wrote her feverish letters, and each was convinced she would marry him one day. Neither knew of the other's existence. She adored being loved that much, and a third suitor would have pleased her that much more. When she took a train to the capital, both of them came to the station to see her off. In order to avoid having to be embraced by either one, she leapt onto the first car she came to. After a moment she went to the window and, in the crowd, saw each of them waving a large white handkerchief, and the look of pleasure that came over her face was taken by both of them as a promise. Stunned by so much desire, she broke with both of them several days later, writing each a long letter filled with confused explanations. She said that the time she had spent with them had been the happiest of her life. Later, when her choice of suitors was more restricted, she chose the federal agent, who promised her a life of banquets in the national capital, where at any moment he was to be transferred. Instead, they had ended up in this miserable little settlement, and to pass the time she had taken up her former job of teaching and had also returned to singing in the choir on Sundays and feast days. She would never again have to choose, she said. In the end, her hesitation had served her well.

We became lovers shortly after her husband began picking quarrels with me, sending me warnings that I must conform to this or that regulation. She loved seeing me as the victim of an unjust government, and because of that she took my side. People in the area hated all governments, only tolerating them as the good passive anarchists they were. She was very happy to see that her husband was persecuting me out of love for her. It was he who, in a peculiar way, drove her into my arms.

All I can say about her is that she was a fairy queen who conspired against all the banalities of existence. I loved her so much that I still to this day refuse to think of her by name.

One fine day she came into my house with a package. Inside was her green dress with the white collar and the fine shoes she'd been wearing when I first saw her. Without a word, she took off her clothes and donned the dress and shoes. "Do you like me better like this?" She understood me completely.

It was the first time in my life I'd been with a woman of a higher station than me, but there was not the slightest suggestion of inequality between us. We were just a man and a woman together—nothing to reproach us, and nothing to stop us either. A lot of nothing, it was true, but it was a nothing that contained everything.

I still think of her as the only woman I've ever loved, because with her, for the first time in my life, I admitted to having a desire for class. Before her, I had been like the little gleaner, who had settled for so little. Loving this woman elevated me. When she was with me, I was no longer ordinary, my mind had never been clearer, and I had the impression that she understood my every thought. With her, I was finally able to accept myself for what I was. I wanted to be with her forever, to have a past with her in it, to cast my anchor for good. Before meeting her, I'd never wanted to be fixed in one place, I'd had too much nostalgia for the happy childhood I'd spent with Salomé and my adoptive family, and I was certain that trying to restore that lost paradise would be a hopeless task. But there, suddenly, I believed it was possible not only to restore the past but to make it better. From then on, I felt capable of rising above myself, of loving higher than myself, higher than anything I'd known before, freely, in the simple joy of being alive.

Her vocabulary reminded me of Salomé. The first time she let me sleep with her, she said: "Call me *tu* with your hands." I got a hard-on that lasted two days. Other times she would say: "Taste me. I'm going to taste you too." She didn't like the expression "make me come," which she thought was vulgar. She preferred to say: "Make me come alive."

Desire gave her a scent that made my head swim. She would have liked being less down-covered, but I loved the tufts of silky reddish hair that peeked out from her armpits and her pubic mound. They made me want to migrate into her body and inhabit it until the end of time. I knew that her body was a utopia, and that I was a mere country, but there was so much gratuitous happiness between us that I never thought of the fates that were watching over us.

Of course, our affair was common knowledge. In such a small settlement, everything was out in the open. She remained living with her husband, who never spoke another word to her and kept sending me warnings, requests, and threats. She read his letters to me lying naked on my bed. When I threw them in the fire, she laughed like a child playing a trick on someone who deserved everything he got. Sometimes I found his threatening letters in the privy, cut up for one final use. Amidst all this fun, I came to believe that the agent could never do me any real damage. She, on the other hand, was less sure, especially when she returned to earth shortly after I'd made her come alive.

I think I let her know we could always leave together, the two of us. We could make a fresh start, a new life, somewhere else. But she never really seemed willing to leave. I sensed her hesitation. She gave me all sorts of excuses, all of them muddled and defeatist: there was the question of her marriage contract, her dowry, the law; she was afraid of losing her teaching position, of being stuck in some public schoolroom for the rest of her life. Her haughty lies were little more than delicate covers. In fact, she didn't want to be with me forever, only once in a while. She loved me, yes, but from above, as a woman who knew that she could always do better. One day she said to me: "Every time I've made a choice, I've made the wrong choice." Her words wounded me, and I lowered my eyes. She quickly tried to excuse her blunder: "I don't mean with you. I don't feel as though I've chosen you. I found you, I went to you of my own free will, and you are still here. I feel so good with you that I don't even dare admit it to myself." She smiled and was quiet, but I knew that the end was near.

She was even more desirable when she was getting dressed. I can't think of anything more beautiful than a woman getting dressed after having sex. At such times she would talk to me, and the nearness of desire, provoked or assuaged, awoke in her a suite of philosophical feelings. Mostly they were thoughts that had already come into my mind but that I could never translate into words. She would put the words in my mouth. I was happy to leave them there, and never let them out of my head.

Once, when she was standing at the window looking out at the fading summer, wearing nothing but her little round spectacles, she said in a melancholy tone, "Freedom is always conditional. And justice is only dished out when it serves no purpose." That's the last time I heard that tone in her voice. She dressed with a haste that I found displeasing. It's the only unpleasant memory I have of her.

I should never have believed we were possible. Our union could only have been one of flight. For her, I was never meant to be more than a passing fancy. There was no misunderstanding between us. On the contrary, we understood each other very well: we were a happy misalliance, a secret, nothing more. I couldn't picture us walking arm in arm in a park, in a pretty little village in the spring, feeding the birds. No, never. Wordless romances like ours are found only in books. Even today I wonder how I could have thought otherwise for a single second.

Shortly after that, her husband showed up at my door with a policeman. He had a long list of grievances against me, among them the fact that I had caused him to be denied his conjugal rights. Worse than that, I was not living in accordance with the rules of the settlement. And so on. The poor police officer never once looked at me, as though he would rather have been anywhere else on earth than where he was.

It was becoming serious. The fishing fleet was about to leave and I could easily find a place. I would have liked to have said goodbye to the woman I had finally loved, but there was no way I could get near her. It was as though she was trying to avoid me. I ran into her one day in the general store in Shippagan. There was a press of people, and she looked away when she saw me. I felt ashamed—also hurt. Later on, I preferred to think that she had been protecting me, since we'd been surrounded that day by men who had their own chattel to protect, their own women, and they would have turned against me out of solidarity with the deceived husband. That, at least, was the excuse I invented so that I could forgive her.

Normally, the fleet was away for three months. This time I signed on for another stretch, and I wasn't sure I wanted to return to the settlement even after that—I had lost confidence in us. Then, when I was back in port, I met the former circus horseback rider.

It took me a long time to understand what it was that attracted us to each other, the former horse lady and me. We were made to be together for a time, but to look at us, no one would have believed it, least of all us. The pleasure of love made her do foolish things, and in such moments I was able to forget the woman I loved. But when alcohol loosened her tongue, the words she would spit at me could only cause bad feelings. She screeched questions at me and swore a blue streak. When the booze loosened its hold on her, she would stroke me again as if she'd known me all her life. Such a pattern could only end badly, there was never any doubt about that.

It wasn't her fault I was arrested, but my absence at least ended her torment. My own, however, had just begun.

As I've already mentioned, the officer who arrested me was an old buddy of mine, and he was kind to me. At the station, he took my arrest order out of a folder and explained that I'd been sought in connection with the death of the schoolteacher. "I'll explain it to you," he said.

She had been found hanging from the ceiling of the church. She was wearing my favourite clothing: the green dress with the white collar, the fine shoes. "We know it wasn't you, so don't worry. You were at sea when it happened, we've checked the dates. The coroner has satisfied himself that it was suicide. But there is an inquest under way all the same, and we have a few questions for you. Her husband has brought a complaint against you. It would be best if you co-operated.

"She was pregnant. Three months. Did you know that?... Her suicide is thus also a homicide. But the law isn't quite clear on that point. There was no child, as such, and there's also the question of the father... But some judges and Crown prosecutors have a certain sense of morality... In any case, you have the right to a lawyer... The questioning won't begin until you've found one...

"You'll spend the night here in one of our cells. You're lucky it's empty. Tomorrow you'll be taken to court, where they'll probably assign you a lawyer. See you tomorrow."

My personal effects were taken from me, and they took my belt and shoelaces as well. I didn't eat or drink for three days. I wanted to expiate her death. My lawyer argued for my release, but I felt guilty all the same. I knew I hadn't been the cause of her death; there are a thousand reasons a person will commit suicide, and I was sure I wasn't one of them. But like her husband, and like the justice system, I wanted someone to pay for her pain. It could have been me, it could have been someone else... I didn't care.

The inquest proceeded. It wasn't a real trial, but I remained in custody because of my record. The police were afraid I would disappear, but there was no risk of that. I was too numb even to consider it.

* * *

The lawyer they gave me was friendly enough, a bit on the portly side, and I was told he was highly regarded at the bar. He said he wanted to help me, and he meant it. But before the inquest began, there were some questions he needed to ask me. First of all, my identity. I'd gone by several different names in my life. I'd taken my mother's name, and Papa's, and those of a few of my employers. They weren't too sure of my age either: was I forty-five or fifty? In short, no one knew anything about me. My police officer friend had to establish who I was, and it took him months. He had to turn the province upside down in order to reconstruct my life.

In the meantime, I was transferred to the provincial prison. I was in protective custody but was treated like any other inmate. It wasn't so bad. I even ran into a few old acquaintances there—sailors, lumberjacks, migrant farm workers I'd come across from time to time. It sounds crazy, but I felt at home in the place, at least for the time being. Time enough to pay my debt to her memory.

The proceedings dragged on forever. Each time I appeared before the judge, my lawyer would plead that there was no reason to keep me locked up and I should be released. "The poor woman took her own life, he wasn't even in the area. She may have hanged herself out of despair, but that hasn't been confirmed by anyone. Mr. Justice, as tragic as this affair certainly is, as much as we all deplore the death of this good person, being the cause of a broken heart is not a crime in this country. How is the Crown prosecutor going to prove that this man drove her to kill herself? It's unheard of! Yes, there's also the question of the unborn child...But again, the law is mute on this point. Another sad affair, I agree, but there is no evidence against my client and therefore no reason to prolong his incarceration." The Crown prosecutor would reply that the inquest was justified if only to prevent further crimes of a similar nature, and the judge would demand more time to study the question.

Then an accidental fire destroyed a part of the prison, and I was one of the inmates who helped the firemen put it out. I could have taken advantage of the confusion to escape, but I still felt far too destroyed to do anything like that. Because they were short of space after the fire, I was transferred to Dorchester Penitentiary. I had to fight when I was there to keep from being killed. It was such an evil place that my feelings of guilt were assuaged and I even began to think about escaping. My lawyer urged me to be patient: "It's a nightmare, I know, and unjust, but rest assured we'll get you out of here..."

But he made a major mistake by requesting my transfer to the asylum in Saint John so they could examine my mutism, which had everyone puzzled. He assured me that my stay in the asylum would be more comfortable and shorter.

He was wrong. I saw a doctor maybe two or three times during the four years I was there. There were more pressing cases than mine, and because I was in an asylum, the authorities convinced themselves that there must be a reason for it—all they had to do was find it. The first few months, I was drugged the whole time. Then I slowly became what they called rehabilitated, to the extent that I succeeded in flattering the guards and the nurses by feigning obedience in all things. It was either that or be killed.

The simple truth was that they had forgotten about me. The judge had ordered me to be released from the asylum, but the Crown had appealed, and time passed. My lawyer died, the judge retired, and the Crown prosecutor was transferred somewhere else. The asylum knew nothing about anything that happened on the outside, and kept me there because no one told them not to. I was caught in a machine that didn't know what to do with me.

There was another truth at play here, but no one spoke of it: the judicial machinery ground to a halt over this business because it had to punish a man who loved a woman who was so beautiful he would never find another like her, and who, even worse, belonged to a higher class than him. By punishing the tramp that I was, a man who had dared to let himself be loved by his better, they would in some way be restoring the memory of the deceased, who was no longer someone who had committed suicide but someone who had had suicide thrust upon her. They would be confirming the rights of her husband over her. Where there had been order, she and I had sown disorder, and so order had to be restored. And for all that to happen, they needed a villain, and there I was. I fit the bill.

It was the war that got me out of that jam. Suddenly they needed space for returning soldiers who were suffering from shell shock. They'd been at the Somme, or Ypres, they'd been in Flanders — names that meant nothing to me. They sent us a doctor who had an easy treatment for light cases like mine. All he had to do was ask: "What's this one in for?" No one knew. My file was empty. He examined me and ordered me released. My patience had paid off.

You might say that the heart of the machine stopped beating for me. The husband of the woman I loved had died, no one remembered that she had been beautiful for me, my land had been repossessed, I had at last paid for my crime of loving outside my own class. The machine could therefore spit me out into the world. It was more economical that way, and it made room for others the machine preferred to eat.

I didn't leave in anger, I didn't file a complaint. I accepted my share of the blame in the sense that I had submitted to the injustice of my own free will, out of my own sense of guilt over the woman I loved. We're like that where I come from. We bow to the force of the machine, but when the machine either winds down on its own or finds someone else to grind to dust, we straighten up, we learn to stand on our own two feet. We don't try to build a sense of dignity out of the memory of our own indignation.

It was around this time that I squatted in the cabin at Cape Enrage, where I lived by selling or bartering my homemade liquor. The rest you already know.

But I have one good memory of my time in the Saint John asylum. Just one.

They called it the Art Hour. Each week, a few soulmates got together in one of the smaller rooms to make art. It had been started by a male inmate who called himself a polygraph: he wrote down everything everywhere, mostly on the walls —poems, songs, essays, the first chapters of novels, fables, treatises, epigrams. He started doing this early in life by writing on the walls of his parents' house, then on those of the school he went to, and from there he graduated to the walls of barns, prisons, churches, villas, inside as well as outside. It was an irrepressible need in him: whenever he saw a wall, he had to write on it. At first he was given only small fines, which gradually became larger fines, until eventually he was put in jail when his writings became subversive, obscene, or defamatory. After that, they threw him into the asylum, where he pursued his literary career on the walls of the bathrooms and outbuildings. A director who was a more creative thinker than the rest came up with the idea of giving him a blackboard and some chalk, and putting him in a sun-filled room once a week to let him write as much as he wanted on the board, after which he could erase it and write more the next week. That calmed him down considerably. Obviously, I couldn't read what he'd written, and his explanations of what he'd put down often confused me, because he spoke at hallucinating speed.

He started Art Hour in order to gather together what he called "the best minds of the house." All the men and women who liked the arts could join him, one afternoon a week, and do what they liked. I don't know why, but every day we went there was sunny. Some of us sang, others recited poetry. There was one woman who painted landscapes that were somehow sad and beautiful at the same time. There was a man who played the piano, always the same piece, but he played it well, and for hours on end. There was another who always showed up dressed as a doctor and pretended to give consultations. He was an actor, I think. And when someone thought to bring a record player and play records, there I was, the dancer, twirling around with my imaginary partner in my arms, who sometimes looked a lot like the woman I loved, other times like the little circus rider. I also danced with Nanna, or Salomé, but not as close, since it wouldn't have looked good.

To honour the initiator of Art Hour, we called him the Maestro, at least those of us who could talk did, and accorded him all the respect due to that title. We even bowed to him. We could see it pleased him. It was during Art Hour one day, one very fine day, that the guards came into the room and told me to go to the front desk to pick up my seaman's bag: I was free to leave. I immediately stopped dancing. The Maestro stopped writing in the middle of an epic and smiled at me. "Bravo, dear colleague," he said. The others applauded.

I didn't know what else to do, so I kissed everyone who was in the room — on the mouth, to show them how much I loved them, because I did, and that I was happy, because I was. I started with the women, of course, out of politeness, and then it was the men's turn, which made the guards laugh. One of them even whispered: "Faggot!" The Maestro was furious. "Hey," he said, "show some respect. Watch your tongue, or I'll write your names on my blackboard!" The whole room exploded in a release of centuries of bitter, pent-up anger, and the guards began backing away. I cut short my goodbyes and left with them.

I still see myself standing outside the gate, wearing the worn-out clothing I'd had on when I was sent to the asylum. Nothing was missing from my bag, my whole former life was in there: the money I'd earned on the boats, my last lead soldier, the signet ring given to me by the woman I'd loved, my beret, my harmonica, my leather-bound book of stories.

The sun hurt my eyes. I was starving, I remember, but I had nothing to eat. The minute I took my first step as a free man, all the memories came flooding back like an old wound. I recognized in the former circus rider — the one who smelled of horse manure and practically loved me to death — the little gleaner Salomé had loved and in whose memory I have never uttered a single word. It was her, it couldn't have been anyone else, with her raging love of life, her unquenchable thirst, her troubled loneliness. I saw her standing with her head bowed, staring down at the floor at her tortoiseshell comb that the constable had smashed with the heel of his boot. I wanted to shout out, like my mother: "Andromache! Andromache!..." To remind myself that it is for her that I have spent a lifetime without words.

The road awaited me, patiently. I stepped out into the setting sun that was burning into my eyes, blessing my sadness.

Andromache...

Maybe it was then that I decided to give up women. I haven't been with one since. Desire, attraction, they're still there, but I don't want to love anyone or be loved by anyone anymore. My memories are all I need.

PART SEVEN

The big day is here. It's a fine day, but I can smell the fog coming in.

The husband borrowed a horse and wagon from his neighbour; he didn't want me to walk all the way to Cap-Pelé since it would make me sweat, and he wanted me to look as good as possible in case I went first. My future depends on how I look—it's as though I were applying for a job. I think there's another motive for his concern as well: he doesn't want to look poor when he arrives at the auction. I represent what's left of his dignity, the dear man. He wants to leave a good example to his successor. So it's for his own good as well as mine that he shows such regard for my comfort.

His wife says it's time. We leave. It's already hot, but the wind is cool and the weather is perfect. The children are gathered on the porch. The eldest hands me my suitcase. She hasn't noticed that it is suspiciously light. I packed it myself. I didn't want any help, because I have a plan at the back of my head.

Last Sunday, I stowed a small cache of supplies down by the river, everything I need to live on if I happen to be taken by a family I don't like. Enough food to last me three days in the Kouchibouguac marshes, a small tent I made myself out of waxed cloth, to sleep in and keep the rain and mosquitoes at bay, and a lined fur coat, mitts, boots for the winter, and things I'll need for fishing and setting snares. I have my money with me, enough to live on for weeks if I'm careful, until I find work in another parish. I could just hide somewhere for a few days to make them think I've left, and then hop a train at the foot of the hill. And from there, the adventure can continue.

I'd like to live in town; it seems to me that I'm ready for it. I'm pretty sure I'd be able to find work, maybe as a night watchman in a hotel or factory. I've been told that's the kind of job they keep for old-timers like me — not too demanding, and you get a lot of time to sleep during the day. I'd find myself a room somewhere, and save enough to have a beer at a tavern once in a while. I'd go to the library to flip through picture books, or to the cinema — there'd be lots of things to distract me. I could go to Montreal, for example. I've never been to Montreal.

Or I could just end my days in the Haute-Aboujagane bush, alone with my memories. Then, too, there's the People of the Sea settlement, in the marsh not far from Sackville — far from here but not too far. I must still know a few people there, and I'm sure they'd take me back. Surely they'd remember me, or at least Salomé.

The sea smells good in the distance. The fruit trees are in blossom. The fog has just settled on the hills around the bay and is spreading out over the sea like a cloud wandering over the land.

* * *

We're the last to arrive. The other two gentlemen being auctioned off are in one corner, sitting on rocking chairs, talking loudly because one of them is deaf. The old woman is alone on the other side of the room, perched on a small straight-backed chair that makes her look alert. The priest has taken on the job of welcoming us in his house, and we are being given tea and spice cake while the preparations for the auction are being made outside.

The priest makes his introductory remarks. We are polite, the four of us, but we know that we are rivals today. This is the first auction for the other three.

I don't know quite what to make of them. They are all older than me. I look at them for faults. The woman's too small, one of the men is deaf, the other talks too much. None of them like the fact that I'm wearing the dead doctor's suit. Those are the only unkind thoughts I can muster while thinking of the children who are at home. They cried when I gave them my blessings.

The woman comes over to join the two others. I'm sitting close enough to hear what they're saying. It's our last stop on the road to death or oblivion. The two old men are talking about their children. One has nine and the other seven, but they all live a long way off, some are even dead. The one who isn't deaf says that he was a teacher in the old days, and he doesn't want his children looking after him; he prefers to die far away from them. The other man nods. The woman looks at me with a dubious smile. She obviously doesn't believe them. Neither do I, and I give her a wink to let her know I'm with her.

The woman gets up and comes over to where I'm sitting. She seems a bit out of it to me, not that it matters. She speaks very slowly, as though I'm the one who's feeble-minded. She says she's heard of me, and she's sure that I'll be going home with a good family. I nod: I don't want to tempt the devil or seem too sure of myself. She insists. I let her know that she's the one who is more likely to go first.

She was a nun almost her whole life. She had to leave the order because of bad health. She was married for a while to a brother who was defrocked too, but in his case it was because he'd lost his faith. They were happy together, she says, but he died two years ago. She has no family, no money, nothing. She hopes she'll end up with someone who has a piano. Sometimes her sentences fail her, though, and it's hard to figure out what she's trying to say. She'll toss out any old phrase to fill the gap in the conversation: "When all's said and done, you know, all this is nothing but a display of good manners." Or: "The future belongs to those who fight."

Suddenly she tells me our auction might be the last one in the area. The new priest finds the custom degrading, and he's let it be known that he'll never condone it. What's more, he won't be with us today; his absence is a kind of disavowal on his part.

I stand up to wish her good luck, and she takes my hands in hers. She gives me her best wishes too.

The crowd is gathered outside, we can hear the noise they are making. There are a lot of them, as I thought there would be. We're sure to find a place, all four of us, unless something unforeseen happens, but we all want the same thing: to have more and better than the others. These little jealousies keep us young, I think.

* * *

The doctor's housekeeper is in the crowd, I saw her car parked in the yard. Maybe she just came out of curiosity, or, worse, maybe she'll take one of the others. No, not that! Her family would rather die than let her spend her last days with a man she picked up at an auction sale. Maybe she'll take the old nun. That would be good of her, and it wouldn't bother me at all. Or maybe she's come for me, and the head-shakers can go to the devil! I've never been able to stop myself from dreaming of beautiful outcomes. It's stronger than I am. This time, I may be dreaming for nothing, which won't be the first time, or the last. Maybe she's given up on men, the way I've given up on women. But that wouldn't stop us from making a happy ending together. We'll see...

It's time. The bailiff calls for silence. The four of us are taken out of the presbytery and made to walk in single file in front of the crowd behind the church. Led by the former priest, we make a solemn procession. Four empty chairs are waiting for us on the makeshift stage. The crowd looks at us. We say nothing.

I think we're making a good impression. No one seems to be feeling sorry for us, which is a good sign. But suddenly, inexplicably, I begin trembling with fear. I don't want to go back to the bush; I don't want to leave the warmth of my familiar places to go live in a strange town. But someone is going to take me anyway, and I'm having a hard time hiding my anxiety. I look over at my companions to try to calm myself. They look tranquil enough, sure of themselves. Their self-assurance gives me back my courage.

The bailiff wants to get things going. Behind us, the fog is already moving in from the sea, in front of us too, in the bush. Soon we won't be able to see our hands in front of our faces.

The auctioneer reads out the names. It'll be too bad for me if the others go to the best families. My fit of anxiety passes as quickly as it came. It's good to be patient. There might be someone out there who sees me in my good suit and has decided to wait until it's my turn before making a bid. What's important, to me at any rate, is that I go for a good price, or at least stay at a respectable level. Not an easy thing. Nothing is certain.

The old nun goes first. She starts at nineteen dollars and goes for fifteen, still fairly respectable. The couple who take her are in their fifties. Something tells me she'll be fine with them. Congrats, madame, I say to myself, standing up and bowing in her direction. (The people in the crowd appreciate this little gesture.) The fog thickens around us. Suddenly I want to play out a few passages from my life for this accidental audience. Do the angel's jig, maybe. But I control myself. I know how to behave, after all.

The silence returns. It's the deaf guy's turn. His file has nothing out of the ordinary in it. Retired farmer. Smokes roll-your-owns and has a bit of money, because he knows how to scrimp. Good health but a touch of the arthritis. He goes down fast from eighteen dollars to twelve. It doesn't seem to bother him that much. Maybe he's used to not showing it. Then the other old guy goes, but I don't hear his price, there's too much noise, or maybe I dozed off for a moment, I'm not sure. I hope no one noticed if I did.

"Silence!"

The auctioneer calls for a short break. I look over the crowd and meet the housekeeper's eye. I think I still might have a chance with her. If I'm not taken by anyone, or if I end up having to run off, I might be able to find refuge with her. That wouldn't be so bad, would it? She likes being looked at, she said, and listened to. I could do that, it wouldn't be all that hard. She likes to tell stories and I make a good audience. In that way, we'd make a good couple.

I give a slight nod in her direction when I see that she's recognized me. She smiles and makes a discreet sign with her hand. I don't smile back, it would seem out of place. I try to maintain a dignified air, like the men you see in old photographs.

To keep myself calm, I think again of the people who brought me into this world: Andromache... Salomé... It helps.

The auctioneer has just said my name: "... Fidèle à Salomé..."

Now it's up to me.

ACKNOWLEDGEMENTS

The only scholarly article dealing with the auctioning of orphans and the elderly is by Grace Aiton, "The Selling of Paupers by Public Auction in Sussex Parish," published in *Collections of the New Brunswick Historical Society*, vol. 16 (1961), pages 93-110. (It is to this article that I owe, among other things, the story of the little gleaner.) The writer Anna Girouard has also taken an interest in the subject, and made it the basis of a series of children's books. It was after hearing about these works nearly twenty years ago that my imagination set to work.

The eminent specialists in Acadian history Régis Brun and Ronnie-Gilles LeBlanc, both with the Centre d'études acadiennes at the Université de Moncton, were of invaluable assistance when I dropped by to see them in 2010. They told me what they knew, and when they gave me to understand that I wouldn't find much documentation about the auctions, I thanked them and left with a happy heart: what I already knew was enough to get under way.

Friends and acquaintances have enriched my story with memories of their childhoods or of those bygone days. I owe a deep debt of gratitude to Andrée Charron, Suzie LeBlanc, Diane Richard, and above all to my wife, Monique Léger.

The rest is fiction.

DANIEL POLIQUIN is one of Canada's leading francophone writers. His novels and translations have won or been shortlisted for several major awards, including the Governor General's Award, the Grand prix du Journal de Montréal, the Prix littéraire Le Droit, the Trillium Book Award, and the Giller Prize. He is also a Chevalier de l'Ordre des arts et lettres and a Member of the Order of Canada. He lives in Ottawa.

WAYNE GRADY is one of Canada's premiere literary translators. He has translated fourteen works of fiction from French by authors such as Antonine Maillet, Yves Beauchemin, and Danny Laferrière. He won the Governor General's Award for his translation of Antonine Maillet's *On the Eighth Day*.